The Bridesmaid's Gifts

GINA WILKINS

MILLS & BOON™

Pure reading pleasure

First published in Great Britain 2008
Large Print edition 2008
Silhouette Books Limited, Eton House,
18-24 Paradise Road, Richmond, Surrey, TW9 1SR

© Gina Wilkins 2007

ISBN: 978 0 263 20111 6

Set in Times Roman 17 on 20 pt.
35-0208-59037

Printed and bound in Great Britain
by Antony Rowe Ltd, Chippenham, Wiltshire

GINA WILKINS

is a bestselling and award-winning author who has written more than seventy novels for Harlequin and Silhouette Books. She credits her successful career in romance to her long, happy marriage and her three extraordinary children.

A lifelong resident of central Arkansas, Ms.Wilkins sold her first book to Harlequin Books in 1987 and has been writing full-time since. She has appeared on the Waldenbooks, B. Dalton and *USA TODAY* bestseller lists. She is a three-time recipient of a Maggie Award for Excellence, sponsored by Georgia Romance Writers, and has won several awards from the reviewers of *Romantic Times BOOKreviews*.

For Kerry

Chapter One

"So you're the psychic."

Aislinn Flaherty had to make a massive effort to hold on to her pleasant expression in response to the drawled comment. She was doing this for her best friend, she reminded herself. Nic was so happy about her engagement, so pleased to be entertaining her future brother-in-law for the first time. Aislinn was going to do everything in her power to get along with him, even though she already suspected that it wasn't going to be easy.

"Someone has obviously been pulling your leg," she said lightly. "I've never even pretended to be a psychic."

"Hmm." Ethan Brannon was visibly unconvinced. Whatever he had been told—and Aislinn intended to grill Nic about that when they were alone—he apparently believed that she did, indeed, make claims to some sort of extrasensory abilities.

She had met Ethan only ten minutes earlier when she'd arrived at Nic Sawyer's house for this small dinner party. After introducing them, Nic and her fiancé—Ethan's brother, Joel—had moved into the kitchen to finish the dinner preparations, leaving Aislinn and Ethan to chat in the living room. This was Ethan's idea of a conversation starter, apparently.

In an attempt to dispel some of the awkwardness, she moved across the room to an antique buffet in one corner of the room. Nic had set the buffet up as a bar, and had encouraged Aislinn and Ethan to help themselves to a before-dinner drink while they waited. "Can I get you any-thing?"

"Yeah, sure. Whatever you're having."

She poured a glass of white wine for herself, a Chivas for him. Carrying both across the room, she handed him his glass. He frowned, looking suspiciously from the drink to her. "Parlor tricks?"

Sipping her wine, she lifted an eyebrow, then lowered the glass. "I beg your pardon?"

"I asked for whatever you were having, and you brought me my usual preference. I suppose Nic told you what I like?"

"Nic and I haven't talked about what you like or don't like to drink," she said, her brusque tone meant to hide a sudden wave of discomfort. "You just don't look like the white-wine type to me."

Still looking at her, he lifted the glass to his mouth.

Despite the inexplicable antagonism she had felt from him from the start, she couldn't help noticing that his was a particularly nice mouth.

He looked very much like a more sharply planed version of his younger brother. Both had crisp brown hair with a slight tendency to wave, clear hazel eyes and strong chins. Both were just under six feet and solidly built. Yet there was a…well, a hardness about Ethan that seemed to be missing in his more easygoing younger brother.

Ethan was three years the elder. A self-employed small-business consultant, he lived in Alabama in a house that Nic had told her was rural and rather isolated. This was his first visit to Arkansas, though his brother had lived here for almost two years. Having met Ethan eight months ago, Nic seemed to like her future brother-in-law, but she had admitted that he wasn't the easiest man to get to know.

"Joel says Ethan was born grouchy," she had confided with a laugh. "But he's actually quite nice."

Aislinn was reserving judgment on that.

"It was generous of you to offer to help Joel

and his partner make their clinic run more efficiently," she said with a determined smile. "They're both wonderful pediatricians, but Joel claims they're both a little challenged in the business-management area."

Ethan shrugged. "I advised Joel to take some undergraduate business courses, but all he wanted to take were science classes. He spent so much time preparing for medical school that he forgot to prepare for the business of being a doctor."

"And that's what you do—teach small-business owners how to make their operations more profitable."

He nodded as he took another sip of his drink.

"Joel told me you're very good at your job. He said you've helped a lot of people stay in business who would have had to declare bankruptcy if they hadn't hired you. He said some of them have actually become wealthy."

He shrugged.

Aislinn swallowed a sigh. She had spent the

day decorating a four-tier wedding cake with a couple of hundred tiny sugar roses entwined with frosting ivy vines. As tedious as that had been after a few hours, it was still less work than trying to draw conversation out of Ethan.

What a relief when Joel came back into the room to announce that dinner was ready. Both Aislinn and Ethan jumped to their feet with almost humorous eagerness to follow their host into the dining room.

Nic was just lighting the candles in the center of her mother's big mahogany table. She had been living in her widowed mother's house for more than two years, since Susan Sawyer had moved to Paris to live with her son, Paul, a U.S. Embassy employee. Nic had met Joel when he'd bought the house next door. Friendship had blossomed into much more, and now Nic and Joel were planning their wedding, which would take place in only a few days.

Taking her seat at the beautifully set table, Aislinn studied the happiness gleaming in her friend's dark-blue eyes. Though Nic had been dating someone else when she met Joel, Aislinn had never expected Nic's relationship with Brad to last. Yet she'd had a feeling from the first time she had seen Nic and Joel together that the two were meant for each other. She hadn't said anything to Nic at the time, but she had done her part to nudge them together—with obvious success.

They talked about wedding plans as they began to eat, Nic sharing a few anecdotes about how difficult it had been to choose the colors and flowers and music and menus for her upcoming wedding. "I had no idea there was so much involved," she added with a groan. "I thought all I needed was a dress and a minister, but people kept adding things to my list."

"What people?" Ethan asked.

"My mother, mostly. She'll be here tomorrow, but in the meantime she's been making long-distance wedding plans and she calls to update me three or four times a day.

Sometimes she forgets the time difference and she calls in the middle of the night to suggest a brilliant idea she just had. And then there were my friends at work, who all had suggestions they thought I should be thrilled about. And my friend Carole, who volunteered to co-ordinate everything during the ceremony and immediately turned into a wedding-planner tyrant."

Ethan shrugged. "You should have told them all to butt out. If you wanted just a dress and a minister, that's all you should have."

Nic wrinkled her nose in a good-natured smile. "It isn't that I mind so much. Everyone knows I'm hopeless when it comes to these girlie things, so they were only trying to help. There were just so many decisions and details. It was mind-boggling at times, but I think it will all work out. I kept it as simple as possible."

"Seems like a lot of trouble. You're just as married if you elope to a justice of the peace as you are after one of these fancy ceremonies."

This time it was Joel who responded to his brother's cynical observation. "That's true, but most people like to celebrate the occasion with friends and family. Nic's mother would have been terribly disappointed if we didn't make a bit of fuss—and, for that matter, so would ours. You know she's looking forward to it."

Aislinn was especially glad for her friend's sake that Joel's mother had endorsed the wedding. Elaine Brannon had made little secret of her reservations about the match when she had first met Nic eight months earlier.

She'd made it clear that it wasn't because she had anything against Nic personally. She had been concerned because Nic was so very different from her son's first wife, a super-model-beautiful, socially conscious family counselor who had died in a tragic car accident less than a year after she and Joel were married. Elaine had wondered if her pediatrician son could be content with an impulsive, sometimes reckless small-town police officer who couldn't care less about being on the social A-list.

Once Joel had convinced his mother that he couldn't imagine being content without Nic in his future, Elaine had given her full approval to the match. All she had wanted, she assured them, was for Joel to find the happiness he deserved in life. If that was with Nic, then she was a welcome addition to the Brannon family.

Ethan mumbled something that seemed to imply that the mother-pleasing argument was no more likely to influence him than ordinary peer pressure.

"So you're saying when you get married, you just want a no-frills elopement?" Nic asked him with a grin.

He set down his fork and reached for his drink. "Marriage isn't on the agenda in my case. I've told you before that I can't imagine finding anyone who'd put up with me for long—or vice versa."

Aislinn's immediate reaction to that assertion

was a vague feeling that he was wrong. Ethan would find someone, she sensed. And it would be a lifelong union.

She couldn't have explained how she knew that fact—and she did accept it as fact, since during her entire twenty-eight years she could count on one hand the number of times she had been wrong when her predictions had been accompanied by a particular feeling. It was not ESP, she had always insisted to anyone who questioned her. She just had better-developed intuition than most people.

Maybe she just paid more attention to her feelings, maybe she was just better at interpreting them—or maybe she was just a really good guesser. But she wasn't "different."

When they had all finished their chicken parmigiana, Nic rose to serve dessert. Reaching for plates, Aislinn offered to help.

"So?" Nic said when they were alone in the kitchen, loading plates into the dishwasher. "What do you think of Ethan?"

Aislinn shrugged. "He's okay, I guess. A little aloof."

"I agree that he's reserved. But underneath, there's a nice guy. He's been very accepting of me, even when his mother was still trying to convince Joel that I was all wrong for him. And he's obviously fond of Joel, very supportive and protective—which, of course, I find sort of endearing."

"He seems to be suspicious of me—as if he thinks I'm trying to run some sort of a con on his family."

Reaching into a cabinet, Nic shrugged. "He's just naturally cautious around new people, I think. He acted a little suspicious of me at first, too. Not rude or confrontational or anything. Just wary. Reserving judgment until he knew what my motives were. Maybe he's been burned a few times."

"A few." It was more a confirmation than a guess. She didn't have the details, but she knew he'd been hurt.

Maybe Nic was right. Maybe that was the reason Ethan tended to be cautious. She would try to be patient during the getting-acquainted process. For Nic's sake. And if it turned out that she and Ethan still didn't like each other after the wedding, it was no big deal. He'd go back to Alabama and they would rarely see each other again.

A funny feeling went through her with that thought. Oddly enough, she had no clue of what it meant that time, if anything. It was just a…well, almost like a mental shiver. Probably nothing at all, she assured herself.

She noticed that Nic was scooping whipped cream onto the first of four bowls of what appeared to be chocolate lava cake. "Leave the whipped cream off one of the desserts," she advised absently.

Nic didn't even blink at the suggestion. She simply loaded three whipped-cream-topped desserts and one without topping onto a tray. "Will you bring the coffee carafe?" she asked over her shoulder as she headed for the dining room.

The Brannon brothers were involved in a discussion of billing practices when Nic and Aislinn rejoined them. Aislinn poured coffee while Nic set the dessert tray on the table. "Is there anyone who doesn't like whipped cream?"

"That would be Ethan," Joel said with a grin. "He hates whipped cream."

Nic smiled at Aislinn before handing Ethan the untopped dessert. "Then I'm glad we left one plain."

Ethan gave Aislinn a hard look, but he didn't say anything as he dipped into his dessert. Concentrating on her own, she hoped the awkward evening would end soon.

Ethan was more than ready for this dinner party to be over. He didn't much care for dinner parties anyway, being the barbecue-and-beer type himself. He wasn't really into wedding planning, though he understood why Joel and

Nic were preoccupied with that sort of thing now. And then there was the psychic....

Not that anyone had ever actually called her that. Joel and Nic had actually gone out of their way to avoid the label, claiming that Aislinn didn't like it. She simply had "feelings," they had assured him. She'd been gifted with a heightened intuition that made it wise to pay attention when she made predictions.

As proof, Joel had pointed to an accident Nic had been involved in while spending a few days in Alabama for Joel's high school reunion. It had been eight months ago, the weekend when Ethan had first met Nic. Aislinn had called Nic's cell phone several times during those few days with vague warnings of impending disaster.

As far as Ethan was concerned, it was simply an unfortunate coincidence that Nic had, indeed, been injured that weekend in an incident that had narrowly missed being tragic. There was no way Aislinn could have known a balcony would collapse beneath Nic's feet, sending her plunging twenty feet to the ground below.

If Aislinn *had* been psychic, she'd have been a lot more specific than saying something "bad" was going to happen, right? Even if so-called precognition existed, what good was it if she hadn't been able to stop her friend from being hurt? So far, all she'd done this evening was guess that he liked Chivas and hated whipped cream. Big deal.

Her alleged extrasensory abilities weren't the only thing about Aislinn Flaherty that made him uncomfortable, he had to concede. Joel had told him that she was very pretty, but that had been a major understatement. Aislinn was gorgeous.

He didn't know why she felt the need to pretend to have supernatural abilities. Surely it wasn't an attention-seeking ploy, since a woman who looked like that could attract all the notice she wanted. She certainly didn't dress for attention; she wore a modest beige knit top and brown pants that were rather plain in themselves but didn't at all detract from her own natural beauty.

As far as he knew, she hadn't asked for any money for her "services" from Nic or Joel— which didn't mean she wasn't conning other people. Perhaps it simply amused her to see how gullible others could be. Or maybe she sort of believed it herself, which was even more pathetic.

Reaching for his coffee, he hoped he would be able to make an escape as soon as dinner was over. He'd been sociable for about as long as he could manage.

"Good morning, beautiful."

The woman who called herself Cassandra looked up from her knitting with a smile and an instinctive little preen. She simply couldn't help reacting that way to young Dr. Thomas, with his warm green eyes and roguish smile. Even though she was old enough to be his mother, there was still enough of the flirt in her to respond to a good-looking man. And besides, this one was special.

"Hello, handsome."

Walking with a rolling gait that was deceptively lazy, he crossed the room and propped one hip on the windowsill near her chair. She liked to sit here in the afternoons, where she could look out at the beautifully manicured grounds and watch the birds nesting in the trees outside her second-story room. She had always loved spring, with its whispered promises of fresh starts and new lives. Even if those promises inevitably died in the cold darkness of winter.

"I've been told you had a difficult night."

Her smile faded in response to his gentle words. She looked down at her knitting, hiding her expression from him as she nodded. "Nightmares."

"They're getting worse again?"

"Not all the time. Just occasionally."

"Do you want to tell me about them?"

Her needles clicked in the silence that followed the invitation. After a moment she said simply, "I don't remember."

"Cassandra."

She could tell by his tone that he was disappointed she had chosen to lie to him. While she was sorry about that, she didn't want to talk about the dreams. About the faces that haunted her days as well as her nights. The memories that were simply too painful to dwell upon, much less to share.

"You have a date tonight," she said instead. "She's pretty, but she isn't the one. You're wasting your time."

Though she could tell he wanted to focus on her nightmares, he indulged her with a slightly strained smile. "You've been listening to the nurses gossip again, haven't you? I swear, you can hardly sneeze in this place without everyone knowing about it."

She merely smiled and continued to work her needles.

"That's what I get, I suppose, for going out with someone on staff here," he added conversationally. "Hard to keep it a secret. Not that I'm trying. But enough about me. Are you sure you wouldn't like to talk to me about your dreams? It just might help, you know."

She lifted her eyes then, studying him sadly. He was so young. So confident that he had all the answers. About her. About his other patients. About himself. Poor, sweet sap.

"It wouldn't help me," she told him quietly. "But thank you for caring, Dr. Thomas. You have a kind heart."

He didn't seem to know how to respond except to stand and murmur, "Thank you. I'll prescribe a new sleep aid for you to try tonight. Maybe it will help you rest more peacefully."

"Whatever you think best, Doctor."

"I'll see you in a few days, okay? If you need anything at all, you be sure and let someone know. I or one of the other doctors will take good care of you."

"I know." She waited until he had reached her door before saying, "Try to have a nice time this evening, Doctor. Despite everything."

He chuckled quizzically. "You're something else, Cassandra."

"You have no idea," she murmured after he'd let himself out. And then she turned her attention back to the garment taking shape in her lap.

Chapter Two

Four days after the dinner party at Nic's house, Aislinn stood at the front of a small church, a bouquet of spring flowers clutched in her hands. As the traditional wedding ceremony began, she glanced toward the best man. A strange sensation coursed down her spine when she saw that he was studying her in return.

She looked quickly away, trying to focus on the minister as he spoke about the joys and responsibilities of marriage. But the uplifting message couldn't hold her attention. Her gaze turned again to Ethan, handsome and remote in his stark black tuxedo.

He wasn't looking at her now, but she sensed that he was still aware of her. Probably wondering why she kept looking at him.

She couldn't have explained. She was simply having a hard time looking away, for some reason.

"Do you take this man…?" the minister intoned, and Aislinn forced her attention back to the ceremony. Her part was coming up.

"I do." Nic's voice was strong and steady as she gazed into her groom's eyes. Eyes, Aislinn noted, that looked exactly like those of the best man—a thought that almost made her look his way again. She restrained herself with an effort, focusing almost fiercely on the bride and groom.

"I do." This time it was Joel who spoke, proudly and confidently. Joel was almost amusingly impatient to begin his new life with Nic and he made no attempt to hide his feelings.

It was time for the exchanging of the rings.

As maid of honor, Aislinn had been responsible for holding the groom's gold band. She took Nic's bouquet, passing the ring to her at the same time. For just a moment they smiled at each other, their long years of friendship forming a bond that let them say a great deal to each other without words.

And then Nic turned to her new husband, and Aislinn was aware of the faintest pang of regret, almost as if an era were ending. She and Nic would always be close, she knew—but it would be different now. Nic and Joel would share a long, happy life together, one that would eventually include a child. A boy who would look exactly like Joel.

Though she had known for a few weeks now, Aislinn hadn't shared that tidbit with her friend. After all, it was only a feeling. A guess, really. And even though Aislinn's "feelings" had an impressive record of accuracy, there were times when it seemed best to keep them to herself.

She glanced once again toward Ethan, who

was watching Joel and Nic now. Strange how she'd had so few insights about him since she had met him. As well as she usually read people, she'd gotten very little from Ethan— primarily that he seemed suspicious of her and had from the start. She still wondered what he had been told about her.

Ethan took great pride in being a realist and a skeptic. He didn't believe in mind readers, mediums, poltergeists, UFOs, vampires, Santa Claus or love at first sight. If he couldn't see it, feel it, touch it or prove it, he had no use for it.

And yet—every time he looked into Aislinn's exotically shaped near-black eyes, he felt something shift inside him. He couldn't explain it any better than that, but something definitely happened. And he had been on edge ever since he'd met her.

Lust, he told himself. Nothing more compli- cated than that. And who could blame him? On a scale of one to ten, this woman was a twelve. A perfect heart-shaped face framed by long, glossy black hair. Eyes as dark as still water on a cloudless night. A full, soft mouth that could make a man want to believe anything she might tell him.

As for the rest of her, well, he had to remind himself that he was in a church just to keep his eyes from lingering too long on curves that made his mouth go dry and his palms itch.

Realizing the fanciful direction his thoughts had taken, he had to force himself not to scowl. He didn't need to be standing up here glowering during the ceremony or people might get the idea he had a problem with the bride rather than the maid of honor.

It was too bad, really. Under normal circumstances, he might have been happy to spend some time with a beautiful woman like Aislinn while he was visiting the area.

It seemed appropriate that her bridesmaid dress was a bold, bright red. The color of danger.

"...I now pronounce you husband and wife."

The solemn words brought Ethan's attention back to the ceremony. He managed a slight smile as Joel enthusiastically kissed his bride to the accompaniment of sentimental sighs from the guests gathered to witness the occasion.

He was as pleased for his brother as everyone else was. Despite his initial concerns about police officer Nic Sawyer's suitability for Joel, he had quickly been convinced that they were a very good match. Though she couldn't have been more different from Heather, Nic was exactly what Joel needed now, six years after the tragedy that had changed the direction of his life. She made Joel happy again, which was all that really mattered as far as Ethan was concerned.

Beaming like two high-intensity bulbs, Nic and Joel turned to face their audience as they were introduced for the first time as Dr. and Mrs. Brannon. Holding her bouquet again in her right hand, Nic slipped her left hand beneath Joel's arm for their walk down the aisle. Following the instructions he had been given, Ethan moved to stand behind the couple, presenting his arm to Aislinn.

She hesitated only a moment before sliding her hand beneath his arm. The pause was so slight that he doubted anyone else had noticed, but he knew he hadn't imagined it.

Despite his skepticism of anything resembling premonition, he had the oddest feeling as he escorted Aislinn down the aisle in the wake of his brother and new sister-in-law. Had to be hunger, he told himself. Lunch had been a long time ago.

Aislinn had practiced walking out on Ethan's arm during the rehearsal the evening before. She had been surprised then to feel such well-defined muscles beneath the conservative but casual business-consultant clothing—and she was struck again now by how strong and solid his arm felt beneath her lightly resting fingertips.

Funny how nervous she'd been about touching him each time, she thought as she smiled at familiar faces she passed going down the aisle. Whatever inspired her hunches, she had never been overly influenced by physical contact. Yet she had been so wary of touching Ethan, almost as if she'd been worried that doing so would trigger some previously unknown ability within herself. How silly.

Or maybe the reason for her hesitation had been a lot more basic than that. Maybe it had more to do with the fact that she found Ethan Brannon just a bit too attractive for her own peace of mind. Dropping his arm the moment they stepped out of the sanctuary and into the vestibule, she reminded herself that he didn't seem to like her very much. She wasn't particularly fond of him, either, with his cutting remarks and obvious suspicions.

"Oh, my gosh." Nic looked a bit dazed as

she turned to Aislinn. "I think I just got married."

Aislinn laughed, as did everyone else within hearing. "You did, sweetie."

"Too late to back out now," Joel said cheerfully.

His bride grinned up at him. "That goes both ways."

Aislinn noted that Joel didn't look at all perturbed by Nic's reminder.

The reception was held in the ballroom of a local country club. It wasn't an overly large room but big enough for the intimate crowd Nic and Joel had invited to celebrate their marriage with them. A local country band, made up of four talented teenagers who were already getting statewide attention for their singing and songwriting talent, provided the music.

Unpretentious but delicious food was served buffet-style, with coffee, fruit punch and sparkling grape juice for beverages. The lack of champagne or other alcoholic choices had nothing to do with the wedding budget but everything to do with Nic's relentless campaigning against drinking and driving. Through her career she had seen entirely too many tragic accidents involving alcohol and she had no intention of contributing to the statistics by serving drinks to people who had driven to her reception.

It wasn't as if public transportation was plentiful in the smallish central-Arkansas town. Whole months often passed without Aislinn seeing one cab. When the locals wanted to go somewhere, they drove. This was part of the reason traffic was such an issue as the thriving area grew more rapidly than the aging street system.

She cast a quick, assessing glance at the table that held the wedding cake, making sure it was still in pristine condition for photographs and the ceremonial cutting by the bride and groom.

Though Nic had requested an understated cake to go with the simple theme of the wedding, Aislinn had spent hours crafting the perfect wedding cake for her best friend. She had taken her inspiration from Nic's heirloom wedding gown, first worn in the mid-1940s by Nic's grandmother, then by Nic's mother, Susan, in the early seventies.

The gown was satin, covered with lace painstakingly dotted with seed pearls. It had been hand sewn by Nic's great-grandmother, making it a priceless family treasure, immaculately preserved. Only a minimum of tailoring had been required for Nic, and Aislinn had no doubt that the gown would survive for another generation or two, perhaps to be worn by Nic's future daughter-in-law, or maybe a granddaughter.

Aislinn had so few heirlooms from her own family that she could only imagine how much the gown meant to Nic and her mother. So the dress had seemed to be the logical theme for the wedding cake. Borrowing Nic's matching veil for a few days and using photographs of the dress as inspiration, Aislinn had designed a white-on-white cake that looked as though it was covered in the same lace as the dress.

It had involved hours of eye-crossingly intricate string work and hundreds of tiny, hand-set edible "pearls." She had created gentle folds in the fondant "fabric" and had cascaded a spray of white-frosting roses entwined with green-tinted frosting ivy down one side, as if a bouquet had been carelessly laid upon the satin-and-lace cake. She'd forgone the overused bride-and-groom topper, using white gum-paste roses instead.

She had been pleased with Nic's reaction upon seeing the finished cake for the first time. Nic had acted as though she had never seen anything more beautiful in her life, even becoming uncharacteristically misty as she had examined every angle of the cake.

"It's gorgeous, Aislinn," she had said huskily.

"The best you've ever done. I feel as though you should enter it in a competition or some-thing, not just give it to me for my reception."

Laughing, Aislinn had shaken her head. "There's nothing I would rather do with it," she had assured her friend. "As far as I'm con-cerned, this is the most special cake I've ever created because it's for you."

The guests at the reception seemed to be properly appreciative of the effort. They gathered around the cake, oohing and aahing, asking Aislinn repeatedly if all the details were actually edible. Laughing, she assured them that, as intricate as the decorations were, the cake was meant to be eaten.

"So you made that?"

She turned to find Ethan standing behind her, a glass of punch in his hand, his gaze focused on the cake. "Yes, I made that."

If he noted her wryly mocking repetition, he ignored it. "It looks nice."

Feeling a little petty now, she replied more

genuinely, "Thank you. It was the most important cake I've ever done."

"You and Nic are pretty tight, huh?"

"We've been friends for a long time. Since
elementary school."

"And when did you start the psychic thing?"

She counted mentally to ten, then gave a
fake smile and a slight wave aimed toward a
pillar on the other side of the room. "If you'll
excuse me, Ethan, I see someone I should say
hello to. Perhaps you should offer your mother
another glass of punch. She looks a little
wilted."

Before he could answer, she was already
moving away, congratulating herself on her re-
straint. There was absolutely no way she would
do anything to put a damper on Nic's wedding
reception, but Ethan Brannon could try the
patience of a saint.

She didn't know what it was about her that
made him feel compelled to bait her, but he
never seemed to miss an opportunity. Fortu-

nately she could think of no reason for spending any more time with him once this evening was over.

"Ethan."

Having been unaware that his brother was anywhere nearby, Ethan grimaced a little before turning around to face Joel with an expression of feigned innocence. "Hey, bro. Nice party."

"Yes, it is. So stop trying to mess it up, okay?"

"I'm not doing anything," Ethan muttered into his punch glass.

"You were picking on Aislinn again."

Faintly amused by his brother's wording, Ethan shrugged. "I was just talking to her. You know, making small talk. Isn't that what one's supposed to do at these things? I told her I liked the cake."

"There was more to it than that. I didn't hear what you said, but I could tell she didn't like it."

"So are you into mind reading now?"

"Leave her alone, Ethan. She's not a fraud and she's not a crackpot. She's Nic's best friend, almost a sister to her—which makes her, like, an honorary sister-in-law to me now. So be nice to her," Joel ordered sternly.

Ethan sighed. "I'll try. It's just that whole psychic thing. I'm not buying in to it."

"Nobody's asking you to. Certainly Aislinn's not asking you to. She hates when anyone calls her a psychic or talks about her…well, *gifts,* for lack of a better word. Just treat her like you do anyone else. No, scratch that. Be polite to her."

Because it was Joel's wedding day and Ethan was feeling uncharacteristically magnanimous, he said, "I'll work on it."

Joel clapped him on the shoulder. "I appreciate it."

Still looking radiant in her white satin and lace, Nic broke away from the final group of well-wishers who had lingered with her at the end of the reception line Joel had just escaped. "What are you two plotting over here?"

Ethan lightly chucked her chin with the knuckles of his free hand. "I was just commiserating with my kid brother. Now that he's married a cop, he's going to have to toe the line."

"You've got that straight." Nic's sudden tough-girl expression was especially funny considering the delicate lace draping her. "I've got handcuffs."

Looking intrigued, Joel slid his arm around her slender waist. "Maybe we should discuss those…later."

Ethan groaned and looked down at his empty punch glass. "I think I need some more of this fruity stuff. Since there isn't anything stronger."

"Nic. Joel." Nic's mother, Susan Sawyer, hurried toward them, a look of determination on her face, which so strongly resembled her daughter's. "The photographer wants to take a few more pictures of you while the guests are in line at the buffet tables."

Though Nic rolled her eyes a bit, she took Joel's arm and turned obediently with him. "Yes, Mother."

Joel looked back over his shoulder at his brother. "Try to look like you're enjoying yourself, will you? I know you don't like parties—but you could pretend you do."

"To paraphrase a cheesy movie I caught on cable recently—this *is* my party face."

Joel moved on with a resigned shake of his head, leaving Ethan to reflect that when it came to parties, he had always been pretty much hopeless. He didn't do small talk, he wasn't much of a dancer, he was uncomfortable in crowds and he was lousy at pretending to be having a good time when he wasn't.

He stood unobtrusively at one side of the room while the other guests gathered around Nic and Joel or sat at the comfortably arranged small tables to enjoy the finger-foods buffet provided by the caterer. Ethan wasn't hungry, so he remained where he was, watching.

His gaze turned toward the cake table in its place of honor. The cake was so fancy that it was almost a shame to destroy it, he thought, wondering how many hours Aislinn had spent on those incredibly detailed decorations. Hers was an odd business. All that time and effort spent on something so transient. A plain cake tasted just as good as one covered in fake lace and flowers.

Still, as a small-business consultant, he appreciated the fact that she had found a market for her skills and was apparently making a living at it. He wondered idly if she was charging enough for her time, taking full deductions on her supplies and other expenses. If she had a solid business plan to keep her on track to grow and expand her cottage industry.

"You're thinking about work, aren't you?" His mother, petite, blond Elaine Brannon, slipped a hand beneath his arm as she spoke indulgently. "You always get that exact look in your eyes when you're trying to figure out how to make money for someone else. Are you already planning how to restructure your brother's business office?"

"Something like that. How are you holding up, Mom?"

She gave him a look and spoke firmly. "I'm fine. The wedding was lovely, wasn't it? Very simple and sweet."

"It was nice. Nic was right to resist overdoing things. I hate those splashy, overblown, pretentious affairs."

"You're referring to your cousin Jessica's wedding last year?"

He grimaced. "Bingo. The circus with the twelve bridesmaids and four flower girls and two dogs in tuxedos and the white doves and oversize ice sculptures and clowns and horse-drawn carriages and full orchestra and endless speeches by inebriated guests."

"There weren't any clowns," Elaine murmured, though she couldn't refute any of the rest of his drawled description. "I was sorry

I coerced you into going to that one. I knew Marlene and Jessica would go overboard, but I didn't think they would get that carried away."

"Yeah, well, the worst part was that Marlene and Ted are going to be paying for that production long after the marriage is over."

"I'm afraid you're right." Elaine shook her head in disapproval. "Jessica and Bobby have already separated twice, and last I heard, things aren't looking any better for them. Still, Marlene could have made an effort to come to Joel's wedding after we all made the trip to Iowa for Jessica's."

As much as he knew his mother enjoyed family gossip—the reason he'd brought up the juicy topic in the first place—Ethan was bored with discussing his father's sister and her ostentatious lifestyle. "You and Susan seem to have been getting along very well," he remarked, glancing across the room to where Nic's mother stood chatting with the minister.

"She's an interesting woman," Elaine agreed.

"She has some fascinating stories about living in Europe with her son. He has to return tomorrow because of job demands, but she's staying here another week to visit with her friends before rejoining Paul in Paris. She even offered to provide accommodations and guide service if your father and I would like to visit there. Wasn't that nice?"

"Good luck getting Dad to Paris," Ethan murmured. "He would be convinced his practice would collapse and termites would eat the house to the ground while he was gone."

Elaine sighed gustily. "He has to retire sometime, right? He can't keep practicing orthodontia for the rest of our lives."

"You know he would drive you crazy if he quit the practice. But maybe he'll agree to take you to Paris later this summer since Susan made such a nice offer. I'll even promise to check the house every day for termites."

Smiling at the gentle mockery of her

husband's one odd obsession, Elaine said, "Between the two of us, maybe we can talk him into it. I would love to see Paris."

Ethan made a mental note to persuade his father to book the trip as soon as possible. And then, because his mother faced a rather significant medical appointment next week, he tried to assure himself that there would be no reason for her not to enjoy that long-overdue vacation.

"You're sure you don't want me to come back to Danston with you? Because I can come back and reorganize Joel's operations later...."

She shook her head sternly. "You will stay here, just as you've planned. It's the ideal time for you to look over Joel's office procedures and to keep an eye on things while he and Nic are away. I never should have told you about my appointment. If you hadn't happened to be there when the nurse called, I would have waited to tell you when I tell Joel—after I have all the results back."

"Yeah, well, Joel's going to be ticked off

that you didn't tell him sooner, just as I would have been."

She leveled a finger at him in the same gesture she had always used when delivering a maternal order. "Don't you dare say a word to him, Ethan Albert Brannon. I won't have his honeymoon spoiled by worrying about something that will probably turn out to be nothing at all."

He sighed and responded as he always did to that particular tone. "Yes, ma'am."

"They're getting ready to start the dancing." Elaine glanced toward the corner where the band was starting to play again. "Interesting choice of musicians. They look young enough to be high school students."

"They are. I think a couple of them are Joel's patients."

"Really? How odd. But pretty much what I've come to expect from Nic."

"Admit it, you like her."

"More all the time," she confessed with a

smile. "She really is a dear, isn't she? And she loves Joel so much."

"Obviously mutual."

"Oh, yes. He's crazy about her." Looking pensive now, Elaine gazed across the room to where Joel and Nic were moving to the center of the dance floor. "I can't help thinking back to Joel and Heather's big, formal wedding. It was so different from this intimate little affair. Beautiful in its own way but different. And as happy as Joel was with Heather, this seems so much more fitting for the man he is now."

Ethan didn't want to talk about his late sister-in-law tonight, six years after her death. "This *is* who Joel is now," he agreed simply, then changed the subject. "Do you want something to eat? I'll get a plate for you."

"No, thank you. I'd better go join your father. He's starting to give me signals that he's ready to be rescued from Nic's uncle's fishing stories. By the way, you really should ask the maid of honor to dance. I know you don't care for dancing, but it is sort of tradition, you know."

He frowned as he glanced instinctively across the room to where Aislinn sat at a table eating with Nic's mother and brother. "Considering my dancing skills—or lack thereof—she would probably just as soon I didn't ask her."

"Nonsense, Ethan. You're perfectly capable of moving in time to the music. And why wouldn't you want to dance with her? She's very pretty. There's something a little…I don't know…different about her, but I suppose that's to be expected from Nicole's best friend, isn't it?"

Elaine seemed to have no idea just how "different" Aislinn was rumored to be—and not just in Nic's refreshingly unpredictable way, Ethan mused after his mother went off to rescue his dad. No surprise, of course. He wouldn't have known himself had it not been for that incident back in the fall, when Aislinn had called to warn of Nic's impending accident.

It wasn't as if anyone around here ever openly talked about it—not that he'd heard, at least. They simply acted a bit wary around Aislinn, as though they weren't quite sure what to say to her.

Oddly enough, he was sometimes treated the same way back in Danston. As though he didn't quite fit in with everyone else. Though, as far as he knew, no one had ever accused him of having any supernatural abilities.

The bride and groom finished their dance, and everyone else was encouraged to take the floor. With a slight shrug, Ethan moved toward Aislinn. What the heck. It wasn't as if there was anything else to do. And dancing with a beautiful woman—even one who pretended to be a psychic—was more entertaining than just standing there being bored.

Chapter Three

Aislinn was taken completely off guard when Ethan asked her to dance, which perhaps explained why she couldn't come up with a quick and polite excuse to decline. Not that there was any real reason why she shouldn't have accepted, of course, she reminded herself as they moved toward the small dance floor. It was sort of expected for the best man and the maid of honor to share a dance.

She was aware of that same odd hesitation when he turned to take her into his arms, almost a wariness of letting him touch her. She still couldn't understand why she felt that way around him. She'd touched nearly everyone else in this room, shaking hands in the reception line, exchanging brief social hugs with the people she had known most of her life. There had been no unusual flashes of insight, no unprecedented reactions to the physical contact. There was just something about Ethan….

"Why did you look so surprised when I asked you to dance?" he asked as soon as they music began.

Keeping as much distance between them as politely possible, she shrugged lightly before answering, "I just didn't think you would."

Mentally she dared him to make some smart-aleck remark about how he would have expected her to predict the invitation, but to her relief, he let it pass. Maybe he'd gotten tired of making digs about her so-called abilities. At least she hoped that was the case.

"I guess you and I haven't gotten off to a very good start," he said abruptly. "And I suppose that's my fault. I'm not very good at the social thing—meeting people, making small talk. Saying the right things."

"You choose not to be good at it because it isn't important to you," she murmured in return. "You're perfectly capable of making polite conversation when you make the effort."

She was almost surprised when he agreed with her rather than challenge her again. "You're probably right. I just don't choose to make the effort very often."

"I'm not exactly a party animal either," she admitted after a moment. "I prefer small gatherings to large crowds. And I sometimes have trouble knowing what to say to people I don't know very well. So I'll take part of the blame for any awkwardness between us."

"Very generous of you."

His tone sounded more humorous than mocking, so she smiled. "Yes, I thought so."

He seemed to search for something else innocuous to say. "They'll be cutting the cake soon, I guess. Will it bother you to watch them chop it up?"

"No." She was amused by his wording. "Why would it?"

"Well, you must have spent a lot of hours on the decorations."

"That's my job. I charge well for my time—though I made this one as a gift to Nic and Joel."

"Nice of you. Do you run your business out of your house or do you have a bakery with helpers?"

"I recently leased a small shop because I'd outgrown my kitchen at home. I have two part-time employees for baking and deliveries, but I do most of the work myself. I prefer it that way for now."

"As good as you are at it, you could probably build up a pretty decent business. Hire a few more people to do the mixing and baking while you concentrate on the arty part. Maybe teach a couple to decorate in your style for everyday orders, saving yourself for the really complicated stuff. You could advertise in Little Rock and online, get your name out there...."

Laughing a little, she tilted her head to look up at him, seeing a gleam in his eyes that had nothing to do with her and everything to do with her business. "Hey, just because you're here to organize Joel's office, don't make the mistake of thinking I want the same thing. I'm perfectly happy with my little operation and I'm making enough to take care of my needs for now."

"For now, maybe," he agreed, "but what about the future? You should be thinking about—"

"Ethan, this is a wedding reception, not a business conference."

His mouth quirked in a slight smile. "I'm painfully aware of that."

The weak joke passed by her as she found herself staring at his mouth. If just that hint of a smile had softened his expression so much, she couldn't imagine how much a full-blown grin would change him. Though she had a strong feeling few people saw him that happy and relaxed, she wished she could see him smile like that, just once. Only to satisfy her curiosity, of course.

He glanced toward the band. "They're pretty good, considering how young they are."

"Yes. They're going to hit it big," she agreed absently, still thinking about Ethan's smile.

He was quiet for a moment, then asked, "Was that just a guess?"

Feeling the muscles of her stomach tighten, she nodded coolly. "Of course. They're very talented. Why wouldn't they be successful?"

Aislinn knew very well that they were listening to a young band who would eventually be stars in their genre. A guess? Maybe, though without the doubt that usually accompanied a shot in the dark. *Intuition* was a more comfortable word for her—one she found easier to accept. Whatever lay behind her occasional predictions, she had enough experience with them to know that she was rarely wrong.

None of which she had any intention of discussing—especially with Ethan, who had made his doubts about her very clear.

She was rather relieved when the song came to an end. She stepped away from him with a bright smile. "I guess I'd better get back to mingling."

He nodded, his own expression unreadable as he studied her face. "I'll walk you back to your table."

Because she didn't want to rebuff him when he was making an effort to be sociable, she nodded and fell into step beside him. On the way back to the corner where she had been sitting with Susan and Paul, they passed a table at which Ethan's parents sat chatting with the minister and his wife.

Elaine Brannon smiled approvingly at Ethan as they walked by, and Aislinn suspected that

Elaine had pretty much ordered her older son to participate in the party. Had his mother been the reason he had asked her to dance?

Glancing at Ethan, she noted the expression in his eyes when he looked at his mother and she caught her breath. There was something she suddenly wanted to tell him, but she hesitated, knowing how he would react.

Maybe she should just keep her mouth shut. After all, these feelings of hers came with no guarantees. She and Ethan had just had a pleasant dance, ending on a fairly friendly note, for them. Why make waves now?

She sighed, aware that she was wasting time arguing with herself. After seeing the worry in Ethan's eyes and knowing it was eating at him, she had to at least attempt to set his mind at ease.

"You don't have to worry about your mother, Ethan," she murmured, turning to him just before they reached her table. "She'll be fine."

His brows dipped into a frown. "What are you talking about?"

"The tests will be clear," she continued quickly, before she changed her mind. "The mass is benign—nothing to be concerned about. So try not to worry too much about it."

"How did you—?"

"It's just a feeling I have, okay?" Anxious to get away from him now, she turned toward the table. "Thank you for the dance, Ethan. I'll see you."

He caught her arm. "Aislinn…"

Maybe it was because she hadn't braced herself this time. Hadn't been prepared for the touch. But she felt the jolt of reaction run through her, all the way from the contact between his hand and the skin of her arm to someplace hidden very deeply inside her. A place she had never wanted to examine very closely herself.

Something changed in his expression, irritation replaced instantly by reluctant concern. His hand tightened around her arm. "Aislinn? Damn it, you've gone white as a sheet. What's going on?"

"I—uh—"

"Aislinn?" Nic appeared suddenly at her other side, looking quickly from Aislinn to Ethan. "Is anything wrong?"

"I—" Abruptly brought back to the present, she looked around, relieved to see that no one else seemed to be looking at them. Not at the moment, anyway. "I think I need some fresh air. If you'll excuse me…"

"I'll go with you."

Aislinn forced a smile for her friend and spoke brusquely. "You'll do no such thing. This is your wedding reception. Go find your groom and dance again. I just need a couple of minutes alone. You know how I am when a lot of people are around."

Because she did know, Nic backed off. "All right. Let me know if you need anything."

"I will."

Without looking at Ethan again, Aislinn made her escape, wishing she could go straight home but knowing she had to stay a while longer yet. For Nic.

* * *

Ethan woke early Sunday morning with that sense of disorientation that usually accompanied waking in a strange bed. It took him only a moment to remind himself that he was in his brother's guest room, the only occupant of the house since Joel and Nic had left after the reception for a weeklong Caribbean honeymoon—the longest either of them could take away from their demanding careers. Ethan would stay here until they returned, at which time—assuming everything at Joel's office was running smoothly—he would head back to Alabama.

Joel had invited his parents to stay at the house, too, but they had chosen to stay in a nearby hotel instead, planning an early departure this morning. Their father was eager to get back to his routines. It was going to take a lot of persuasion for Elaine to get him away for that European vacation she longed for, Ethan thought with a shake of his head. Lou Brannon was the very epitome of a contented homebody. Something Ethan understood a bit too well.

Glancing at the clock on the nightstand, he saw that it was just after seven. Yet he'd bet his parents were already on the road. His dad liked to get an early start.

So here he was, the only member of his family in a town where he hardly knew anyone. During the five days he had been here, he'd spent several hours at Joel's clinic, meeting the partner and staff, looking over the operations with an eye toward streamlining bookkeeping and maximizing profits. Joel and Bob were literally putting their business into his hands.

He and their newly hired office manager, Marilyn Henderson, would meet with several software salespeople during the next week, as well as have long discussions about existing office practices. They would pore over the books and filing systems, deciding what to change and what to leave alone—though there would be very little of the latter.

Joel and Bob were great guys and excellent doctors, but neither of them had paid much attention to the business part of the practice they had opened just under two years earlier. They could definitely use some help in that area, and Ethan already had a plan in mind. Fortunately Marilyn seemed to be in agreement about the way a pleasant yet efficient medical office should be managed.

Since he was alone in the house, he pulled on a pair of jeans and zipped them but left the snap undone. Barefoot and shirtless, he wandered into the kitchen, yawning and wondering what Joel had left for breakfast. He found orange juice in the refrigerator and poured himself a glass, then popped a bagel into the toaster. Only then did he admit that from the moment he'd opened his eyes he had been trying without success to forget about Aislinn Flaherty.

He had every intention of avoiding her for the remainder of his stay in Cabot. Shouldn't be too hard. He doubted that she would visit the pediatric practice. And he wouldn't be ordering any cakes.

He'd given up trying to decide if she was crooked or crazy, but her comment about his mother's upcoming medical tests had made a cold chill go down his spine. He'd known for a fact that no one knew about those tests except his parents and himself. Just to confirm, he'd casually asked his mother afterward if she had mentioned the situation to anyone else. Anyone at all.

She had reminded him that she wanted to keep the tests absolutely secret until after she learned the results. She had been especially adamant that Joel was not to be told until after his honeymoon.

So how had Aislinn known?

He knew that so-called psychic con artists performed what were known as cold readings—throwing out vague comments and then watching carefully for the most minute changes in expression and subtle body language from their gullible marks. But as far as he'd been able to tell, Aislinn hadn't prefaced her remarks about his mother's health with anything he would have considered fishing for clues. And she hadn't spent much time talking alone to either of his parents, so he kept coming back to the same question....

How had she known?

Not that he had changed his mind about her alleged abilities. Guess or guile, she hadn't just pulled that prediction out of the ether. And while he fervently hoped she was right about the tests resulting in good news, he would consider it no more than a happy coincidence if it turned out to be true.

Just as well he wouldn't be seeing her again anytime soon, he told himself as he finished his breakfast. He was just too uncomfortable around her, for quite a few reasons.

Someone rang the front doorbell, startling him as he set his dishes in the dishwasher. He pushed a hand through his tousled hair and moved toward the front door. He couldn't imagine who would be at Joel's door on a Sunday morning when everyone knew Joel was out of town. Maybe his parents hadn't gotten that early start after all.

Having no psychic abilities of his own, he was surprised to find Aislinn on the other side of the door. She wore a gray T-shirt, jeans and sneakers, her dark hair pulled into a loose ponytail, no evidence of makeup on her striking face. She looked as though she had crawled out of bed, thrown on the first clothes she'd found and driven straight over. "What are you doing here?"

She didn't appear to take offense at the blunt greeting. "I need to talk to you."

"What about?"

She sighed. "May I come inside?"

For only a moment, he hesitated, tempted to close the door in her face. He finally stepped aside, not because he didn't want to be rude but because he didn't want to think of himself as a coward.

"Okay," he said, facing her from several feet away, his arms crossed over his bare chest. "What is it? Another 'prediction'?"

She looked around the room, her expression distracted, and then she turned and moved toward the hallway. Frowning, Ethan dropped his arms and followed her. "Where are you going?"

Without answering, she turned left, into Joel's bedroom rather than into the guest room on the right where Ethan had been staying.

"Aislinn, what the hell are you—"

"There's a photograph," she said vaguely. "I need to—oh, here it is."

The small, framed photo sat on top of a bookcase in one corner. The paperback mysteries Joel liked to read to relax at bedtime filled the bookcase almost to overflowing. On the wall above hung a framed watercolor painting of a peaceful lake cove surrounded by trees and boulders. Joel was the artist; until Nic had told him a few months earlier, Ethan hadn't even known Joel liked painting with watercolors.

"You sure know your way around Joel's house," he muttered as Aislinn picked up the photograph.

"I've never been inside this house before," she replied absently. "We've always gathered at Nic's instead."

So how had she...? Shaking his head impatiently, he told himself that he had no way of judging if she was even telling the truth. "Okay, what's going on?"

She drew a deep breath and looked at him. He noted abruptly that she still looked as oddly pale as she had when they'd parted last night. Perhaps that was why it was no surprise when she warned, "You aren't going to like this."

He was pretty sure that would prove to be an understatement.

Aislinn had been too focused on finding the photograph to pay much more than passing attention to Ethan when he'd let her in. She'd managed maybe two hours of sleep last night before she had finally given in to the overwhelming urge to drive to Joel's house. She'd waited as long as she could, doubting that Ethan would appreciate being awakened before dawn so she could find a photograph that was haunting her. Not that he'd been overjoyed to see her as it was.

Only now did she really look at him. He, too, seemed to have only recently crawled out of bed. His hair was mussed, he hadn't shaved and he wasn't wearing a shirt or shoes. His jeans weren't snapped. A stark contrast to the tidy and tuxedoed groomsman she had seen the evening before, she thought.

She wondered if it was weird that she thought he looked even better like this than he had at the wedding. More natural. This was the real Ethan—and despite his forbidding expression, he was a very attractive man.

Pulling her gaze away from the well-defined

muscles of his lean chest and abdomen, she moistened her dry lips, her fingers tightening around the small silver frame clutched in her hands. She wasn't exactly sure how to begin, since she already knew he wasn't going to believe a word she said.

"Well?" he prompted impatiently.

Might as well stop stalling. She turned the photo toward him. "You recognize this picture, of course."

He glanced at it, then shrugged. "It's my family, obviously. Some thirty years ago."

"Your father. Your mother. You." She pointed to each figure as she named them. Ethan was perhaps six in the photograph, maybe seven. She indicated the younger boy next to him. "And this is Joel."

Ethan nodded, a muscle clenching in his jaw as they both turned their attention to the baby sitting in Elaine's lap.

"Who is this?"

For just a moment she thought he wasn't

going to answer. And then he muttered, "That's Kyle. I assume you already know he died when he was almost two."

"Can you tell me what happened?"

He crossed his arms over his chest, making the muscles bulge just a little. If he was trying to look intimidating, he succeeded. Of course, he also looked sexy as all get-out, but she couldn't think about that right now.

"Why do you want to know?"

"Please, Ethan. Just humor me for a few minutes. I know this must be difficult for you."

"It happened a long time ago," he said with a slight shrug. "I hardly remember him."

It took no special ability at all for her to know that he was lying. She looked at him without responding.

After a moment he shook his head and spoke curtly. "He drowned. It happened during the aftermath of a tropical storm. There had been a lot of flooding, a lot of local destruction, and even though the weather was still bad, Mom had gone out with one of her charity groups to try to help some of the people who had suffered the most damage to their homes. Dad was at his office, making sure everything there was okay. They left Joel with the nanny who took care of us while Mom was busy with her volunteer work, which was pretty often back then."

"And there was an accident?"

He nodded. "Joel and I were spending the week with our maternal grandparents in Tennessee, as we did every summer while they were living. Mom thought Kyle was still too small to be gone for that long. Anyway, for some reason, the nanny took him out during that heavy rain. No one knows why they left the house. They were in her car, a cheapie little compact."

He cleared his throat, then continued, "Apparently she hydroplaned, went off the road and was swept into a flooding river. The car was found a few days later, overturned in very deep water, but it was empty. Several other people drowned during that same tropical storm and resulting flood. There was another man whose body wasn't recovered for several months, but neither the nanny's body nor my brother's was ever found."

There was no identifiable emotion in his tone, though his eyes looked darker than usual. He obviously believed every word of the sad story he had just told her. The story that had been told to him.

She moistened her lips again. "It isn't true," she whispered.

He frowned more deeply at her. "What isn't true?"

"Any of it. I mean, I know that's what you think happened. What you all believe. But…"

Ethan's arms dropped to his sides, the fists clenched. He took a step toward her, making her instinctively move backward. "If you're going to try to feed me a load of crap about how you've been talking to my dead brother…"

"No!" She shook her head forcefully. "It's

not like that, Ethan. I'm not a medium. And even if I were, it wouldn't apply in this case."

"And just what is that supposed to mean?"

She drew a deep breath, then blurted out the words before she could lose her nerve. "Kyle isn't dead."

Chapter Four

A gentle breeze ruffled Cassandra's snow-white hair, one straight lock tickling her right cheek. She reached up to tuck it back, savoring the scent of the flowers that bloomed in the gardens around her.

As she often did, she thought of how fortunate she was to be at this pleasant, exclusive, private facility. It was expensive, but her late husband had made sure she would be well cared for after his passing. Just as she had known he would when she'd married him.

She sat alone in her little corner of the garden. She didn't mingle much with the other residents here, most of them being quite a bit older. Besides, she wasn't interested in socializing. She actually enjoyed her solitude, for the most part.

She didn't come outside very often, but she had allowed herself to be persuaded this afternoon, thinking that the fresh, warm air might clear her mind. She didn't like the new medications. They left her feeling groggy. Lethargic. And she still had the nightmares. Not as often, maybe, but just as vivid and disturbing when they came.

She would have to ask Dr. Thomas to make another adjustment.

Her knitting needles clicked with a slower-than-usual rhythm as she tried to immerse herself in the soothing sounds of the birds singing in the trees above her head, the water splashing gently in the nearby fountain. Lovely, peaceful sounds that almost—but not quite—drowned out the echoes of her dreams.

"Here you are."

She couldn't have said how much time had passed between her thoughts of him and his appearance. A few minutes. An hour, perhaps. Time had a trick of slipping away from her. "Hello, Dr. Thomas."

He sat on a concrete garden bench, crossing one leg over the other. The casual pose stretched the fabric of the khaki slacks he almost always wore with a solid-color shirt and brightly patterned tie beneath the required white coat that made him look so handsome and professional. She liked the way he dressed. Not too stuffy but neatly enough to show regard for his patients here.

There had been a trend away from ties and white coats a couple of years ago, but the residents hadn't liked seeing their physicians in blue jeans and polo shirts and other members of the staff in T-shirts and flip-flops. Now that the doctors were back in their white coats and the rest of the staff wore tidy uniforms, everything seemed to run much more smoothly. More civilly. She firmly believed that the general decline in polite society could be measured by the pervasive loss of respect for proper attire.

And weren't there people in her past who would find that attitude hilarious, coming from her?

"What are you thinking about so seriously?"

She made herself smile as she replied candidly, "Neckties and panty hose."

To give him credit, he didn't seem at all taken aback by the non sequitur, asking merely, "Are you for 'em or agin 'em?"

She chuckled, thinking of how much she liked this nice young man. "I'm for 'em."

He tugged lightly at the blue-and-green-patterned tie he wore with a blue shirt that contrasted nicely with his light tan. "I was afraid you might say that."

Laughing again, she shook her head. "Don't try to con me. You like looking nice or you wouldn't give so much thought to matching your shirts and ties. Unlike some of the doctors who show up in mismatched patterns and colors that make one's head hurt to look at them."

"Now, Cassandra, don't make fun of Dr. Marvin. Everyone knows he's color-blind."

"Then he should always let his wife dress him in the mornings, bless his heart."

Grinning, the doctor nodded. "You're probably right. So how are you?"

She told him about the effects of the new sleep aid, finishing with a request for a change.

Dr. Thomas nodded gravely. "We'll make another adjustment. I still think it would be good for you to talk about your dreams with someone, though. If not with me, at least with your counselor. We don't discuss specifics about our clients, as you're aware, but I get the feeling you aren't being much more forthcoming with her than you are with me."

"I tell you both everything you need to

know," she assured him, catching a dropped stitch.

"I would like to think you trust me, Cassandra."

The sincerity in his voice was genuine, not like some of the doctors who only pretended to be truly concerned about the residents here. Dr. Thomas cared so much that she was tempted at times to advise him to put a bit more distance between himself and his patients. As appealing as his empathetic nature made him, it also made him more susceptible to burnout and disillusion. As fond as she was of him, she would hate to see him fall prey to either of those conditions.

"I trust you as much as I trust anyone."

He sighed lightly. "I suppose I have to be satisfied with that."

Nodding, she let her hands rest. "How was your date last week?"

"We were talking about you, not me."

She lifted her needles again.

After a moment, he conceded. "We attended a symphony performance. We had a flat tire on the way to the concert hall, but I was able to change it without messing up my clothes or making us late to the concert. On the whole, it was a pleasant evening."

"But a little dull," she interpreted, reading easily between the lines. "You probably won't ask her out again. I told you she wasn't right for you."

He shook his head in obvious exasperation. "Maybe you can introduce me to Ms. Right," he muttered.

"I can't introduce you, but I can tell you that you'll know when you find her. And you will find her."

"A seer, are you?" he teased.

She didn't smile in return.

"You're crazy."

Aislinn flinched in response to Ethan's blunt words. "I'm not crazy."

"Then you must think *I* am. Because there is no way I'm buying whatever it is you're trying to sell."

"I'm not trying to sell anything, Ethan. I just…know."

"You don't know anything." He took the photograph out of her hands and set it a bit too forcefully back into place on Joel's bookcase. "I think you'd better leave now."

She sighed wearily. "I knew you would react this way."

"Did you? Well, hell, maybe you *are* psychic."

He stalked to the doorway, pausing there with one hand motioning for her to precede him. It wasn't a request.

Though she moved past him out of the bedroom, she wasn't ready to completely give up. "If you would just let me tell you what I—"

"I'm really not interested." He kept walking, straight toward the front door, making her have to hurry to keep up with him. "I know Nic thinks the world of you, and Joel seems to like you, too, so I'm giving you the benefit of the doubt. Maybe you really believe the things you say. Maybe you've guessed correctly so many times that you've convinced yourself you really do have some sort of gift. But this time you've taken it too far."

"Don't you think I know how bizarre this sounds?" she retorted. "Can't you understand how hard it was for me to come here, knowing how you would respond?"

"Then why did you come?"

She sighed and pushed her hands into her pockets. "I had to," she muttered. "I couldn't sleep last night and I knew I wouldn't be able to rest until I talked to you about the…about the feeling I had about your brother."

"And just when did you get this … feeling?"

The slight note of mockery behind the word wasn't lost to her, but she answered evenly, "Last night. At the reception. When you touched me, I—I knew there was something I had to tell you. I wasn't sure what it was until later, during the night, when I got…I don't know…some sort of a mental image of this photograph. When I looked at it, when I held it, I knew what I had to tell you."

Ethan's expression didn't change during her halting, stumbling explanation. She swung out her hands in frustration. "I know it sounds crazy! I spent most of the night wondering if I really have lost my mind. I don't have visions, Ethan. I don't get flashes when people touch me. Like you said, I make guesses—and they usually come true. But this is different. This isn't something that has ever happened to me before."

"Really?" He made no effort to hide his disbelief. "How about last year, when you kept calling Nic in Alabama to warn her that something bad was going to happen to her?"

"I told you—that was a feeling. Just a vague sense of uneasiness that made me worry something might go wrong. The sort of premonition ordinary people get all the time."

Ordinary being the operative word. It was all she had ever aspired to be.

Ordinary.

Normal.

He shook his head. "Coming into my brother's house, going into his bedroom, telling me Kyle didn't drown thirty years ago—that's not the sort of thing ordinary people do, Aislinn."

She swallowed. "I know."

Letting his breath escape in a long, slow exhale, Ethan pushed a hand through his hair, leaving it even more mussed than it had been before. "I'm not sure what I should say here. I'm not very good at this sort of thing. Maybe you should get some help. You know, see someone. If you need me to call anyone—a friend, maybe, a family member—just tell me the number."

Oh, great. Now he was trying to be nice even as he suggested that she should be taken away in a straitjacket.

"You know what, Ethan? You're right. I shouldn't have come here," she snapped, moving toward the door. "I should have known how you would react. I *did* know, but I thought I could persuade you to listen. I was wrong about that, but I wasn't wrong about Kyle. He didn't die in that flood. He's very much alive."

He didn't respond, but she hadn't really expected him to. She grabbed the doorknob and jerked open the door. She'd stepped only halfway through when she turned to throw one last reckless comment over her shoulder.

"You want a real, live prediction from a real, live freak? Fine. Your parents are on their way home. They'll arrive just fine, but they'll be delayed by several hours because they're going to have a blowout in a little town just inside the Alabama border. The left rear tire, and it's going to take them a while to have it repaired. So figure out how I 'guessed' that, why don't you? *I* certainly don't know."

She slammed the door behind her with

enough force to rattle the diamond-shaped glass pane in the center. And still it didn't seem hard enough to express the full extent of her anguished frustration.

Ethan was trying his best to concentrate on his work when the telephone rang later that afternoon. Glancing at his watch, he decided it was exactly the time his parents should be arriving safely at their home, probably without any untimely delays at all. "Hello?"

"Hey, bro, it's Joel."

So he'd guessed wrong. "What are you doing calling on your honeymoon? You don't have enough to keep you entertained there?"

Joel chuckled. "Trust me, I've got plenty to do here. I just forgot to do something yesterday and I wanted to ask you to take care of it for me."

"Sure. What is it?"

"There's a stamped envelope on my desk, made out to the American Cancer Society. It's a memorial for one of my patients that I meant to mail before I left—but, well, I got kind of distracted yesterday. I just remembered it and I hate to let it wait until I get back. So would you mind sticking it in the mailbox for me later?"

"No problem. It'll go out first thing tomorrow."

"I appreciate it. So how's everything else? Any problems there in the house?"

"Joel, you've been gone less than twenty-four hours. The place isn't going to fall apart just because you aren't here."

His younger brother chuckled ruefully. "I'm turning into Dad, aren't I?"

"I'm not going to lie to you, kid. You're sounding a lot like him. Now go concentrate on your beautiful bride and quit worrying about things here."

"Nic wants to say hello." He handed the phone over before Ethan had a chance to send his regards through Joel.

"Hi, Ethan."

He answered in patient resignation. "Hi, Nic. Did you forget to mail something, too?"

"No, I think I took care of everything," she replied, missing the joke. "Have you seen my family today?"

"I saw them earlier. Your brother came over to tell me goodbye as he left for the airport. He asked me to keep an eye on your mom's house while I'm here."

"Oh, good. I was going to ask you the same thing."

"I'll tell you the same thing I told them. If your mother needs anything while I'm here next door, all she has to do is ask. She would probably tell you the same thing she said to me—she'll be just fine. She said she expects to be so busy catching up with all her old friends before she rejoins Paul that she won't be home much, anyway. I believe she's at a party of some sort now."

"That doesn't surprise me. So what about you, Ethan? How are you entertaining yourself there?"

"I've been working. Trying to go over Joel's books before I meet with Marilyn and the software people tomorrow."

"That doesn't sound like much fun. You shouldn't work the whole time you're there. I know you don't know many people, but maybe you could call Aislinn? She'd probably be happy to show you around...or something."

Ethan pulled the telephone receiver away from his ear to stare at it incredulously. Was Nic actually trying to fix him up with her spooky friend? He knew they hadn't spent all that much time together yet, but he'd have thought his new sister-in-law would still know him better than that!

"I'm going to be pretty busy while I'm here," he said after a moment. "Joel's billing procedures are a mess."

He had no intention of telling either Nic or Joel about Aislinn's weird visit that morning and certainly not the reason why she'd claimed to have come. He only wished he'd thought to forbid her then to call and bother Joel and Nic on their honeymoon with that wild tale. Surely even she wouldn't go to that length for attention—would she?

It took him a moment to realize that Nic was speaking again, and that she sounded a bit disappointed. "Oh. Well, if you're not interested… But she really is very nice. Like you, she's just a little hard to get to know."

"Oh, I don't think Aislinn's at all like me," he muttered.

"What was that? I didn't hear you."

"Nothing. Look, Nic, you and Joel should be out snorkeling or horseback riding or sailing or something. Don't worry about anything here, okay? Just enjoy your honeymoon."

"Okay, but—"

Joel apparently took the phone from Nic's hand. "We'll talk to you later, Ethan. You know how to reach us here if anything comes up."

"Yeah, I know. Have fun."

He hung up with a frown, hoping nothing would happen to spoil his brother's honeymoon.

Though Aislinn wasn't officially open for business on Sundays, she spent Sunday afternoon in the shop she had recently rented in a strip mall on the outskirts of town. She had a lot to do during the next few days. While it was nice to be doing well in her business, there were times when it all seemed to be moving too quickly. She'd had half a dozen serious inquiries just at the wedding reception.

She was piping a delicate string of yellow frosting when someone hammered on the shop door early that evening, ignoring the Closed sign. Her hand jerked, ruining the effect of the decoration she'd been trying to complete. Swearing beneath her breath, she determined that the damage was repairable before she set her tools aside and went to answer the door.

She passed by the display counter and the table and four comfortable chairs where she sat with clients as they discussed details of their orders. Photo albums of her work were neatly displayed on a small bookshelf, and framed enlargements of some of her best cakes decorated the walls. A few green plants were scattered through the room, but nothing else that would detract from the photos. More out of habit than anything, she glanced around to make sure nothing was out of place.

Though she hadn't been expecting him exactly, it didn't take much effort to figure out who she would find on the other side of the glass door with its drawn shade. "There's no need to knock it down," she said as she released the locks and opened the door.

Ethan dropped the fist he'd been using to knock on the thick glass stenciled with the words *Cakes by Aislinn*. "How did you do it?" he demanded, pushing past her without waiting for an invitation. Once inside, he turned to glare at her. "How did you know?"

She closed the door, knowing it would serve

no purpose to ask him to leave, the way he had kicked her out of Joel's house earlier. "I take it you've heard from your parents?"

"They called me when they got home," he agreed gruffly. "They were running a few hours later than they expected. They had a blowout."

"Left rear tire?"

He nodded without taking his eyes away from her face. "How did you know, Aislinn?"

"What? You don't want to accuse me of somehow sabotaging their tires?"

He shook his head impatiently. "I know you couldn't have done that. But I still don't know how you predicted the tire was going to blow."

Her head was starting to hurt. She rubbed irritably at her left temple as she turned toward the kitchen.

"I need some tea," she said, figuring he deserved the same abrupt treatment he'd given her. "We can talk in the kitchen while the water comes to a boil. But, I warn you, I'm not in the mood for any more of your accusations. You can listen and you can ask questions, but start calling me a liar or a con artist again, and I'm throwing you out on your ear."

It was just as well he didn't ask how she intended to do that, since he outweighed her by some fifty pounds. Still, as grumpy and un-friendly as Ethan had been to her, she wasn't afraid of him. When she wanted him to go, he would leave.

She had leased this shop because of the large, utilitarian kitchen. Big enough to hold a sizable work island, with two ovens, a six-burner gas range and an industrial-size freezer and refrig-erator, it was the place where she spent the most time, even more than she did at her home these days. A small, rectangular metal table sat against one wall, with four simple metal chairs so she and her employees could take occasional breaks.

Ethan glanced at the towering cake on the work island. "Another wedding cake?" he asked, picking up a long, serrated knife she used for torting—slicing layers into thinner layers.

"It's for a golden anniversary celebration tomorrow night," she answered, reaching for the teakettle.

He walked slowly around the island, studying the very traditional cake Aislinn's client had chosen. A lemon cake filled with raspberry jam, it was covered in golden-yellow fondant, draped in icing shells and strings and topped with two entwined translucent golden rings made of sugar. Lovely but quite simple, actually, in keeping with the unpretentious personalities of the celebrants. "It's nice."

It was the same adjective he'd used for the much more elaborate cake she'd made for Joel and Nic's wedding, she remembered. An all-purpose cake compliment, apparently. "Thank you."

She opened a stainless-steel cabinet to take out a mug. "Would you like tea?"

"You tell me."

Closing the cabinet a bit too firmly, she snapped, "I have no idea."

"Sorry," he muttered after a moment. "No, I don't want any tea just now, thanks."

He took a seat at the table, and a short while later she joined him, a steaming mug of chamomile tea in her hand. She set the beverage in front of her as she sank into a chair on the opposite side of the table from him. It wasn't that she wanted the tea so badly; she had simply needed something to do to occupy her hands while she talked to him.

"Okay," she said. "I'm ready to talk."

He rested his forearms on the table and looked intently at her face, as if to watch for any sign that she wasn't being entirely honest with him. "How did you know about the blowout?"

"I don't know."

He cursed beneath his breath, slamming one hand down on the stainless-steel tabletop. "You said you were ready to talk."

"And I *am* talking," she replied defensively. "You asked me a question. I answered honestly. I don't know how I knew. I just did."

"Did it come to you in a vision?"

"I don't have visions."

"A little voice in your head, maybe?"

"I don't hear voices."

"So…?"

"I just knew," she repeated, unable to think of any other way to explain it. "I have these feelings sometimes. And sometimes they come true. I've always believed that everyone has them. Maybe I just pay more attention to them."

"I don't have them."

"Surely you've had odd premonitions. The feeling that something's going to happen. Or the phone rang and you somehow knew who was on the other end. Or maybe you were thinking about someone and then coincidentally ran into them."

"Well, yeah, but—"

"That's all it is with me. Feelings. Intuition. Whatever you want to call it."

"I think you're the one playing with semantics. Intuition doesn't explain the things you've said to me during the past couple of days. No one gets a vague feeling that a near stranger's left rear tire will blow out just over the Alabama state line. That's a little more specific than a good guess."

Her fingers tightened spasmodically around the mug. "I know," she said, her tone sounding rather miserable even to her. "I—it's not usually quite that detailed."

"You said the same thing about your 'feeling' about Kyle still being alive."

A slight tremor went through her, causing hot tea to splash on her fingers. She quickly released the full mug, reaching for a paper napkin to dry her fingers.

"Are you all right?"

"I'm fine," she said without looking at him. "I just spilled a little tea."

Though she was still looking down at her fingers, she knew he hadn't turned his gaze away from her face. "I want to know what made you come to Joel's house this morning," he said, getting to the real reason for this visit. "What did you hope to accomplish with that crazy story about my little brother?"

Chapter Five

This was so much more difficult than Aislinn had anticipated. Even with Nic, she rarely talked about her insights. She simply stated what she thought Nic needed to know, and Nic took the warnings to heart with a matter-of-factness that Aislinn had always appreciated. No comments or questions about how Aislinn had known, just an acceptance that somehow she did. And that she was usually right.

It was one of the reasons Aislinn was so fond

of Nic. Nic had never treated her as an oddity, unlike so many other people they knew.

"I try to avoid the *C* word," she muttered, glaring into her mug again. "I'm not crazy."

"Whatever. So how long have you had these feelings?"

The slight hesitation before the word let her know that he was as uncomfortable talking about this as she was. "A long time. Most of my life."

"And how many people know about them?"

"Only a few," she answered with a shrug. "Though even most of them don't know quite how often it happens."

"You downplay your abilities."

It wasn't a question, but she nodded. "Yes. As it is, there are those who make too big an issue of it."

She thought of her friend Pamela, who sometimes bragged about her friend the psychic, even though Aislinn had asked her repeatedly not to say that. Pamela had a good heart and was a loyal friend, bringsing Aislinn a lot of customers for her cake-decorating business. She didn't mean any harm by her comments; she actually considered it a compliment, since she was fascinated by anything that appeared in the least paranormal.

Aislinn, on the other hand, assiduously avoided any hint of such a thing. She was as normal as anyone else, she had spent her entire life insisting.

"So most of your friends just think you're pretty good at guessing things that are about to happen and take it for granted that they should listen to you."

"Something like that."

"But what they really think is that you're at least somewhat psychic and you just don't like to admit it."

"I—" She stopped, then sighed. "Maybe," she conceded reluctantly, suspecting that was exactly what others secretly thought. Even Nic, probably.

"I don't believe in psychics."

So why did he keep insisting on calling her

that? Shaking her head in exasperation, she said, "I don't care. I'm not sure I believe in them myself."

"What was the point of coming to Joel's house this morning?" he asked again.

She took a sip of her cooling tea, mostly to give herself a moment to put her thoughts in order. "I probably shouldn't have done that," she conceded, setting the cup down carefully in front of her. "I'd had a bad night and I thought if I could just look at the photograph, maybe convince myself I was making too much of it…"

"You'd seen the photo before?" he asked when her voice trailed away.

She shook her head. "No. I told you, I'd never actually been in Joel's house before."

"Then how did you know where you would find it?"

"Maybe I should start from the beginning."

"That's probably a good place to start."

He was still being sarcastic, but rather

absently now, without the aggressiveness of earlier. Almost like a habit he had developed very quickly around her.

Giving him only a mildly chiding look in response, she began, "It happened at the reception last night. You touched my arm—"

"I remember. You went pale. I asked you about it."

She nodded, feeling again the jolt that had gone through her with that contact. She hadn't known what it was then, only that she'd felt almost as though she'd been body-slammed. It was later, during the long, nearly sleepless night, that she had begun to see that portrait in her mind.

Every time she'd tried to close her eyes, she'd envisioned the photograph sitting in Joel's bedroom—and had recognized that bedroom even though she had never stepped foot in it. She'd never experienced anything like that before, but she had been compelled to drive to Joel's house that morning, knowing she wouldn't be able to stop obsessing until she did. It was almost as if her movements had been controlled by some force outside herself, drawing her to Joel's house and then into his bedroom, to the photograph she had seen in her mind.

Only when she had held the frame in her hands had she understood exactly what she needed to tell Ethan. She had looked at the face of the baby boy in the photo—and she had seen the man he had become. Not *would have* become. *Had.*

"I'm sorry, Aislinn, I just can't buy it," Ethan said, shaking his head when she finished. "There's no way Kyle survived that flood. The police found the nanny's car upside down, twelve feet deep in water."

"But no bodies."

"Well, no. It was thirty years ago, after all. Toddler seats weren't as secure as they are now. The seat apparently broke loose."

"And the nanny's seat belt?"

"Undone. Either she wasn't wearing it or she managed to get herself free and was swept away in the deluge. One of the car doors was open."

"Or she was able to get out with the child and neither one of them drowned."

"That's what you think happened?"

She twisted her mug in front of her. "That's what I know happened."

"You just know."

She nodded. "I just know."

"And you expect me to believe you."

She felt her mouth twist in a wry smile. "No."

"Then what do you want from me?"

"Nothing," she replied simply. "I just needed to tell you. What you do with the information, if anything, is up to you."

He brooded about that for a moment, then asked, "So what else do you know?"

"What do you mean?"

"Do you know where this man is? The one you say is my brother?"

"No."

"What about the nanny? Is she still alive? Can you tell me how to find her?"

"I don't know."

"Then what the hell do you expect me to do?" he asked irritably.

She spread her hands. "I'm sorry, Ethan. I keep trying to explain that nothing quite like this has ever happened to me before. I don't know what it means or what to do with it—and I'm almost sorry I said anything to you about it. Maybe I should have just kept my mouth shut."

"No," he said after a moment. "I'm the one you should have told. The only one, by the way. I don't want my parents or my brother to hear about this until I look into it."

"You're going to look into it?"

"I'm not saying I believe you," he responded quickly. "I don't. But I'll try to check it out, if you'll promise you won't say anything to Nic or Joel."

She didn't like the implication that he was

offering to indulge her in exchange for her silence. It wasn't as if she had anything to gain either way. "You do what you want," she said stiffly. "I won't mention any of this to anyone else."

He nodded. "Good."

"So how are you going to begin? Looking into it, I mean."

"Beats the heck out of me. I don't suppose you can do some sort of woo-woo thing and give me a starting point?"

She didn't even bother to get annoyed that time. "Sorry. I'm all out of woo-woo at the moment."

"Guess I'm on my own then."

"Guess so."

But he continued to sit there, looking at her across the table.

Growing self-conscious after a few moments, she asked, "Are you sure I can't get you anything?"

He glanced at the work island, then drawled, "I wouldn't turn down a piece of cake."

Something about the way he said it made her laugh. "I'm afraid that one's spoken for. But as it happens," she said, rising, "I have something that might appeal to you."

"Do you now?"

She faltered for just a moment in her steps, then made herself keep moving toward the refrigerator. No way he'd meant that the way it had sounded, she told herself. Had it been anyone else, she'd have thought he was flirting. But this was Ethan, who thought of her as a crackpot who couldn't quite be trusted. She would be the last woman he would consider flirting with.

She pulled out a cake plate and set it on the counter. She had tried a new cake recipe, making a small, round chocolate cake torted into four layers with caramel filling, then frosted with white-chocolate-flavored butter cream. She had topped the cake with a few yellow-frosting daisies and piped a simple yellow shell border around the edges.

"Do you like chocolate?"

"I consider it one of the essential food groups," he replied. "Especially if you've got a glass of milk to go with it."

She set the cake on the table and opened the refrigerator again. "Of course."

Ethan was studying the cake when she returned to the table with a full glass of milk. "Looks too nice to cut just for me. Did you have plans for this one?"

"Not really. I make small cakes sometimes to try out new recipes. I keep them on hand for walk-in business, people who need a cake for a special occasion but forgot to place an advance order. I get several requests for those each day."

"I guess you get tired of cake for yourself."

"No. I love cake." She served him a generous slice, cutting a smaller piece for herself.

"You must not eat it all that often."

The rather clinical once-over he gave her in tandem with the observation made her shake her head. Did the man have absolutely no tact or did he just rarely bother to make an effort?

"I try to keep balance in my life," she said mildly. "When I eat cake, I exercise a bit more to make up for it."

"Wow. This is good."

The compliment pleased her since it seemed completely sincere. "Thank you. I'll have to consider adding this recipe to my menu."

He nodded, washing down another bite with a sip of his milk. "How long have you been running your own cake-decorating business?"

"Just a couple of years. I started out in high school decorating birthday cakes for a super-market, and it expanded from there as I became interested in more intricate designs."

"You didn't go to college?"

"No." She had no intention of going into her family history with him just then. "What about you? You have a degree in business, I assume?"

"Double major. Business and economics."

"And how long have you been self-employed?"

"Five years. I quit my job with an accounting firm on my thirty-first birthday to open my own business."

"You like being your own boss."

"Right. Just like you do."

She nodded to concede his point.

Apparently out of small talk, he finished his cake, drained his milk, then stood. "Thanks for the cake. I'll let you get back to work now."

"Wait a sec." She crossed to the counter where she'd left the chocolate cake, took out a small delivery box and carefully set the cake inside it. Closing the lid, she turned and held it out to him. "Here. Something for you to snack on while you're staying at Joel's."

He hesitated only a moment, studying the box with her logo printed neatly across the top. And then he accepted the gift with a slight smile. "Thank you."

"You're welcome."

Carrying the box, he preceded her through the shop to the front door. He paused with one foot outside on the sidewalk. "I assume you'll let me know if you get any more, uh, feelings about my family."

"I would have thought you'd want me to keep any future feelings to myself."

He frowned. "Just come to me if there's anything you feel you need to pass along."

She didn't respond.

After a moment, Ethan turned away. "Goodbye, Aislinn."

Closing the door behind him, she thought about the finality with which he had spoken. Ethan wasn't expecting to see her again. And while she almost never had premonitions involving herself, she knew somehow that he was wrong.

"Are the books that badly messed up?"

Ethan blinked and looked away from the computer screen. "I, um…what?"

A curvy brunette in pale blue scrubs leaned against the countertop beside him. "The way you're glaring at that computer, I figure what you're seeing must be really bad."

Clearing the screen, Ethan leaned back in the chair, grimacing when stiff muscles protested. Apparently he'd been sitting there longer than he'd realized. Unfortunately he hadn't accomplished much, since he'd been having a hard time concentrating on the numbers. "It's not so bad. Just a little disorganized."

"Yes, well, Carla Colby set up the books when Joel and Bob went into practice together. Carla used to be the bookkeeper for old Dr. Green before he retired, and Joel and Bob figured she must know what she was doing, but her methods were a little outdated. She retired a few months ago. I think Marilyn's going to be a great office manager once you get all the systems up to date."

"Yes, she's very efficient." He looked around the empty office. "Where is Marilyn, anyway?"

"She went home. It's five o'clock, Ethan. We're closing up for the day."

He glanced at his watch in surprise. Now that he thought about it, he sort of remembered Marilyn saying something a few minutes earlier. Must have been good-night. He hoped he had at least grunted a response—and that she had assumed he was preoccupied by work.

"Guess I let time slip away from me."

Nurse Lizzie Murdoch laughed quietly. "I know when a man is obsessed with his work. I see that look all the time around here with Joel and Bob. But you've got to take a break sometime, you know?"

"Yeah. As a matter of fact…" He pushed himself out of his chair, knowing he would accomplish nothing more by sitting there any longer. "I might as well head out myself."

"Do you have plans for dinner?"

He shook his head. "Joel stocked his kitchen for me. I'm sure I'll find something edible."

"There are some pretty decent restaurants around here, you know. Do you like catfish?"

"Yeah, I—"

"I know—why don't you and I go grab something to eat? I don't have any plans this evening, either, and it's always nicer to eat with someone, isn't it?"

Actually, he was just as content dining alone most of the time. And Lizzie was being about as subtle as a semi with her "spur-of-the-moment" invitation. He supposed she was attractive enough and she seemed like pleasant company. But he wasn't really interested in getting involved with one of Joel's employees during the short time he planned to be in town.

"Just a friendly dinner," she said quickly, as if sensing the direction his thoughts had taken. "Seems only hospitable, since you're a visitor to our town and your brother is away on his honeymoon."

Ethan shrugged. Her tone had reassured him that she wasn't going to expect much from their dinner, and he supposed there was no need to be antisocial. "Okay. Catfish sounds good. You think anyone else wants to join us?"

The expression in her eyes let him know she'd gotten the message. But something about her smile hinted that she hadn't completely written him off. "I'll ask around," she said, "though just about everyone else is gone for the day."

As it happened, he and Lizzie were the only ones free for dinner. They agreed to meet at the restaurant at six-thirty, giving them both a chance to freshen up first. Lizzie had swapped the scrubs for a low-scooped T-shirt and a short denim skirt with high, wedge-heeled sandals when she rejoined him. Even though he couldn't help noticing how nicely she filled out the rather skimpy garments, Ethan kept his behavior politely distant as they were seated at a booth and served fried catfish, hush puppies, coleslaw and green tomato chowchow.

Lizzie kept the conversation moving with talk about the wedding. "It was really nice, wasn't it? Simple. Like Nic. Not that I mean Nic is simple, of course. I meant, you know—"

"Unpretentious."

"Yeah. That's it. So, anyway, everyone thought you and Joel looked so handsome up there in your tuxes," Lizzie continued flirtatiously. "Y'all really look a lot alike, you know?"

"So I've heard." Ethan stuffed a hush puppy in his mouth.

"And Nic looked so pretty in her heirloom gown. All feminine and delicate, which certainly was a change from seeing her in her police uniform all the time around town. And then Aislinn, of course, well, she's just gorgeous no matter what she's wearing."

Ethan took a deep swallow of iced tea to avoiding having to respond.

"The cake was fantastic. Aislinn's had cakes featured in cake-decorating magazines, you know. She did one for my niece's sweet-sixteen party. It looked like a filigreed jewelry box with the lid partially open and a string of pearls spilling out of it. It had ribbons and flowers and glittery jewels—and every bit of it was edible. Made out of frosting and sugar and stuff, you know? Cost my sister a freaking fortune, but everyone said it was worth it. Aislinn took a picture of the cake and put it on her Web site."

"So do you know Aislinn very well?" Ethan asked casually, dragging a strip of fish through tartar sauce.

"I wouldn't say *well,*" Lizzie replied with a shrug. "I don't think anyone knows her well— except Nic, of course. The two of them have been tight since grade school. They were a few years behind me in school," she admitted with a rueful wrinkle of her nose.

"What do you mean about no one knowing Aislinn well?"

"She's just very private. Reserved. A result of her childhood, I guess. I mean, she's nice enough. Her business is pretty successful—lots of word-of-mouth referrals. And you don't hear anybody say anything bad about her. Well, not very often, anyway. There are people who think she's a little spooky. Something about the way she looks at you sometimes, you know? Like she knows something you don't. But personally I think maybe she's just a little shy and occasionally her shyness comes across as sort of distant."

While he would have liked to follow up on that throwaway comment about Aislinn's childhood, he refused to gossip about Aislinn behind her back. He'd found out what he wanted to know already.

There didn't seem to be any general talk about Aislinn being psychic. Just "a little spooky." She'd apparently been telling the truth when she said that only her closest friends knew about her extraordinary intuition.

Which didn't mean he completely believed in it himself, of course. Even if she had been uncannily accurate so far.

And speaking of spooky…

Something made him look up and across the room, toward the cash register. His eyes met

Aislinn's just as she turned, holding a white take-out bag.

She blinked a few times in surprise, then nodded a greeting before turning and walking out the door.

"Ethan?" Her back to the registers, Lizzie hadn't realized that the woman they'd just been talking about had been in the restaurant. "Still with me? You look a million miles away."

He pulled his attention back to the table. "Sorry. I guess I got distracted."

"You really are a workaholic, aren't you?" She shook her head in resignation, and Ethan got the impression that she had just written him off as a potential for anything more than a temporary coworker.

Though he would just as soon keep it that way, he made an effort to be a bit more companionable during the remainder of the meal. Yet he found it harder than he would have expected to put thoughts of Aislinn out of his mind.

* * *

Ethan went straight back to Joel's house from the clinic Tuesday afternoon. Lizzie didn't bother to ask him to dinner again, probably knowing he would have declined if she had.

The phone rang only a few minutes after he walked in. He picked it up, thinking his brother might be checking in again. Instead it was his mother's voice he heard on the other end of the line.

"You can stop worrying," she told him, her tone much lighter than it had been the last time they'd spoken. "The tests came back clear. It's just a little benign cyst. The doctor said I'll be just fine."

Ethan felt relief flood through him. "That's great news, Mom. Must be a load off your mind. Not to mention Dad's."

"Oh, yes, we're both quite relieved."

They talked a few minutes longer about everything her doctor had said that afternoon. And then Elaine said that she had to go. Lou was taking her out to dinner to celebrate, she added.

"Have a good time. Love you, Mom."

"I love you, too, sweetie. See you soon."

Hanging up the phone, Ethan spotted the telephone book lying on the counter nearby. On an impulse, he picked it up. Turned to the *F*s. There was only one Flaherty listed, with the initials A.J.

Even as he dialed the number, he wondered why he was doing it. Wondered what he would say if she answered.

"Hello, Ethan," she said calmly.

Caller ID, he realized abruptly. That invention let everyone sound a little psychic.

Rather than comment about her greeting, he said, "A. J. Flaherty. Aislinn…Jean? Joanne?"

"Joy," she replied.

"I see." A little more frivolous than he had expected. It made him curious again about the veiled comment Lizzie had made about Aislinn's childhood. "I heard from my mother today. The doctor's report came back exactly as you predicted it would."

"I'm glad. I know you were worried about her."

"Yes, I was. I still don't understand how you knew."

She remained silent. Maybe she felt as if there was just nothing left to say in response to his continued skepticism.

"I saw you yesterday," he said. "At the restaurant."

"Yes, I saw you, too."

"You know Lizzie?"

"In passing. She grew up around here, too."

"She works for my brother, you know. We were both free for dinner, so we ate together."

"Okay."

He didn't know why he'd felt the need to explain. She certainly didn't seem all that interested. "So anyway…I just wanted to tell you about my mom."

"I'm glad you called."

"Yeah." An awkward silence stretched through the line, and then Ethan cleared his throat. "So have you had any new visions?"

"I told you—I don't have visions."

"Any new 'feelings,' then?"

"No."

"Nothing more about my supposedly missing brother?"

"Kyle is alive, Ethan." Her tone seemed to say that she knew she was wasting her breath trying to convince him.

Because he couldn't tell her otherwise, he said nothing.

"Thanks again for calling me about your mom's tests," she said after a moment. "If there's anything else you need while you're in town, feel free to call."

He felt as though there was something else he wanted to say to her, but his mind remained frustratingly blank. "Uh. Yeah."

Very smooth, Brannon.

"Goodbye, Ethan." Aislinn disconnected before he could make a further fool of himself.

He supposed he should be grateful for that.

Chapter Six

"Good morning, Cassandra." The nurse entered the room with a broad, fake smile, her voice artificially cheery. She carried a paper cup that held several pills.

Already in her chair by the window, her knitting in her lap, Cassandra made an effort to speak warmly, though this was one of her least favorite of the facility's staff. "Good morning. How are you today?"

"Me? Oh, I'm fine. It's you we're worried about. Did you sleep better last night?"

"A little," she lied, taking the cup and the glass of water Nurse Chirpy handed her. She had pretty much given up hope that her problems could be solved with a colorful little capsule.

As much as nice, young Dr. Thomas wanted to help her, there was little he could do to heal the wounds of her past. But, just to make everyone happy—and because there was always the outside chance she could be wrong about their benefit—she dutifully swallowed the pills he had prescribed for her.

Sometimes Aislinn dreamed about cakes. Some of her best designs had come from her dreams, causing her to keep a pad beside her bed so she could make rough sketches before the elaborate dream designs escaped her. She might have worried about that being a little weird, but having heard that writers and designers described similar experiences, she figured maybe it was relatively normal for creative types to dream up ideas.

She woke Wednesday morning groggy. Not particularly well rested. She could vaguely remember tossing and turning during the night and she thought maybe she had sketched something on her pad, though she couldn't remember exactly what. Probably a cake. Considering that she'd been mostly asleep when she'd drawn it, she doubted that the idea would be worth pursuing.

It was quite a shock to see a man's face staring out at her from the notepad. Drawn with some detail, the face was strong, handsome, appealing. He looked a little like Ethan. A little like Joel. But not exactly like either of them.

Although Aislinn had always thought Joel was nice-looking and she was a bit too attracted to Ethan for her own peace of mind, she had to admit that the man she had drawn was more striking than either of them. And there was no doubt in her mind that this man was their brother, Kyle.

Shaken, she sat on the edge of the bed, staring

at the drawing. She didn't remember sketching the face. But, even more disturbing, she had never shown any talent for drawing portraits. Were she to try, she wouldn't be able to do it again now, wide-awake.

She picked up the phone. "Ethan?" she said a few moments later, hearing the unsteadiness of her own voice. "There's something I think I need to show you."

Twenty minutes later he was at her door. From the look on his face, she must have sounded more disturbed than she had even realized when she'd called him.

"What's going on?" he asked the moment she opened the door. "Are you okay?"

Now that she'd had time to think about it, she rather regretted calling him. Had she been more awake, less perturbed by seeing the drawing, she would have talked herself out of making that call. Ever since she'd hung up the phone, she had been berating herself. She had pulled on jeans and a T-shirt, brushing her hair into a ponytail and forgoing makeup, trying to brace herself for Ethan's disbelief and renewed suspicions about her.

She hadn't expected him to look so worried about her.

"I'm fine." She motioned him into her living room, which was decorated in soft creams and taupe. Soothing colors.

Aislinn's home was her retreat from a hectic world that could be overwhelming to her at times. When she was here, she sought peace and refuge. She rarely even turned on the television. She met with clients only at her shop these days. Only a few close friends spent much time in this sanctuary.

She hadn't expected to invite Ethan here.

"I'm sorry I disturbed you so early," she said, self-consciousness causing her to babble a little. "I had a small shock when I woke up and I called you without stopping to think about it. You told me to call you if I had any other insights about your brother."

His eyebrows dipped downward into a frown as he turned to face her. "You've learned something new? You've had another…what do you call them? A flash?"

"No, I don't call them flashes. I just have feelings." She'd said the words so often they were starting to sound clichéd even to her. She shook her head impatiently. "I made coffee after I called you. Would you like some?"

He looked as though he intended to refuse and then he stopped himself. His expression wry, he nodded slowly. "Yeah. I haven't had any coffee yet this morning. Something tells me I'm going to need it."

"Have you had anything to eat?"

"No. I jumped in the shower to wake myself up and then headed straight over here. You gave good directions, by the way. I had no trouble at all finding your house."

She glanced at his damp hair and pictured him taking a quick shower and throwing on the polo shirt and khakis he wore. Deciding she'd better put all thoughts of that out of her mind if she wanted to be relatively coherent, she motioned toward the kitchen. "At least let me feed you while I talk."

He hesitated, then nodded again. "I could eat."

Like the rest of her house, her kitchen was done in peaceful, earthy colors. A commercial-type refrigerator/freezer, double ovens and abundant counter space remained from when she had operated her business out of her home. She had bought the house specifically for the spacious kitchen, the largest room in her otherwise smallish home.

"Nice," Ethan said, glancing around as he took a seat at the small oak table. "Did you grow up in this house?"

"No, I bought it a few years ago." The down payment had come from an insurance payoff after her grandfather's death. Because that was a long, complicated story, she didn't elaborate. "Do you like oatmeal?"

"Don't know. I haven't had oatmeal since I was a kid."

"Really? I have it quite often. It's what I had planned for my own breakfast this morning. It will only take me a few minutes to make some, if you want to try a bowl."

"Yeah, that's fine." There was a note of impatience in his voice, as if food was the last thing he wanted to talk about just then. "I still don't know why you called me over this morning," he reminded her as she started assembling the ingredients for their breakfast.

She stilled her hands for a moment, then went back to work. "I think I've been stalling a little. I know how you'll react."

"You think you know," he corrected her. "Why don't you tell me and find out for sure?"

She was glad to have something else to do while she talked, so that she didn't have to look at him while she told him about her restless night. About waking to find the drawing on her nightstand.

"It's there," she added. "In that sketch pad."

He picked up the pad she had set on one corner of the work island and turned pages. The first few sheets were filled with cake designs, roughly drawn with little detail, difficult to decipher for anyone except her. He stopped on the sketch of the man's face. "Is this what you're talking about?"

She glanced over her shoulder, then looked away again. "Yes. I don't remember drawing it. I didn't even know I could draw like that. I've never been able to sketch a recognizable face. But when I woke up—there it was."

"Do you know who it is?"

"Yes." She could tell by his tone that he'd already guessed her answer. "It's Kyle. The way he looks now, I mean."

Ethan looked at the sketch for a long time in silence, then set the pad aside. "You understand that I'm having trouble believing this."

"I knew you would."

"So you just sat up at some point during the

night, drew this face in your sleep, and decided this morning that it must be my brother."

"It sounds strange when you put it like that."

"You think?"

She winced in response to his tone, but didn't pause in her breakfast preparations. "As I said, I probably shouldn't have called you. It rattled me a little to see the drawing this morning, and I acted without taking enough time to talk myself out of it. But since you're here, I feel like I should tell you everything."

"Definitely tell me everything."

She carried two bowls of steaming oatmeal to the table, then returned to the counter for a pitcher of milk and small bowls of brown sugar and raisins. Spreading a napkin in her lap, she sat across from Ethan and picked up her spoon.

"As I said," she began, sprinkling brown sugar and raisins into her bowl, "I knew who I had drawn as soon as I saw the sketch pad this morning. But that wasn't all I knew. Which is why I felt that I should call you."

Having heaped a generous spoonful of brown sugar onto his oatmeal, Ethan paused in the process of adding raisins. "What are you talking about?"

"I got a couple of names. Do you know someone named Mark?"

"I've probably met a few Marks in my life, but no one comes immediately to mind."

"What about Carmen?"

Watching him closely, she saw a muscle twitch in his jaw. "What about Carmen?" he asked.

"Who is she?"

"As if you don't already know."

"I don't know," she refuted. "The name popped into my head this morning, and I knew it was important, but I don't know who she is."

"Carmen was the name of Kyle's nanny. The one who disappeared the same day he did."

Aislinn's expression didn't change. Either she had already known the answer to her question—

despite her assertion otherwise—or she wasn't particularly surprised by his response.

Deciding to play along until he could figure out what she was up to now, he asked, "The name just came to you this morning?"

She nodded, dipping a spoon into her bowl. "Mark and Carmen. Both names just kept repeating in my mind. You must think that sounds strange—and, trust me, it feels that way to me, too. I know I keep saying this, but this is all so different for me. So unlike anything I've sensed before."

Yes, she kept saying it. And he still didn't know what to make of it. "I suppose it wouldn't have been that hard for you to find out the name of Kyle's nanny. Old newspaper reports of the storm and its victims, maybe even something Joel let slip one time."

"Joel never talks about your brother's accident. Neither Nic nor I knew anything about it until we'd known him for almost a year—when she went to Alabama with him for the reunion. He has never mentioned the nanny at all."

While she obviously resented his implication that she had looked up the information she claimed had simply come to her in her sleep, she managed to keep her irritation in check. Only her slightly clipped tone let him know how she felt about his comment.

"I didn't say you did look it up. I merely pointed out that you could have," he said mildly. "Is that all you have? The two names?"

She started to say something, then fell quiet, nodding as she ate another spoonful of her oatmeal.

He swallowed a bite of his own, savoring the creamy, brown-sugar-sweetened taste. It was good. Much better than he remembered from childhood. Either his tastes had changed or Aislinn cooked oatmeal better than his mother had. Didn't mean he could believe anything she told him, of course. "What were you going to say just now? Before you changed your mind."

"I—nothing."

He set down his spoon. "Aislinn, I may not be psychic, but I can tell you're holding something back."

She sighed and pushed her half-empty bowl away. "It's all mixed up in my head," she admitted. "I don't like sounding like a flake when I've never thought of myself that way. Before now, everything I've felt or guessed seemed so…I don't know, normal. Maybe a little more intuitive than most people but nothing too far out of the ordinary. To be honest, I worked pretty hard at maintaining that illusion. Keeping some of my feelings unsaid, even with Nic, drawing little attention to myself, putting all my energy into my cake-design business. And then you came to town."

"And what exactly changed when I came to town?"

She motioned toward the sketch pad, still open to the drawing of the man she said was Kyle. "That, for one. I really can't draw like that. If you asked me to draw a face now, I wouldn't be able to. Not with that kind of detail. And I've got to tell you, it creeps me out to think of myself sitting up in the night drawing in my sleep like some sort of zombie."

Her wording might have been amusing had he not identified a bit too closely with the distaste in her voice. He suspected he would have felt much the same way had he been presented with evidence that his actions had been controlled by some outside force. He was way too much of a control freak to be comfortable with that image.

"And then there were the names," she continued, her hands clenched into fists on the tabletop. "Mark. Carmen. Carmen. Mark. Just hearing them over and over in my mind, like when you get a snippet of music in your head and it just won't go away. That's what those names became to me. Annoying and repetitious."

"I can ask my mother if she remembers anyone named Mark. Maybe Carmen had a boyfriend. Or a brother."

"Maybe." But neither of those explanations seemed to completely satisfy her. After a moment, she shrugged. "It would be a start, anyway."

"You can't give me any other leads?"

She shot him a quick glance, as if trying to determine whether he was making fun of her, and then she replied, "Just one other possibility."

"Which would be?"

"The state of Georgia has some connection to your family."

"Georgia," he repeated.

She nodded.

"I've never been to Georgia. As far as I know, my family has no connection to the state. We lived in North Carolina before we moved to Alabama."

"I don't know what the connection is. Just that your search will eventually lead there. Whether it will end there, I don't know."

Having nothing else to say about that at the

moment, Ethan finished the last of his oatmeal, then set his spoon in the empty bowl and reached for his coffee. "That was good. Thank you."

Clasping her hands in front of her, she nodded. "You're welcome."

He drained his coffee cup and set it next to the bowl, giving himself a moment to choose his words. And then he looked somberly at her across the table.

"I still don't know exactly how to get started, but I'll look into all of this," he said. He had told her that before but had yet to make the first inquiry. Probably because doing so would have felt almost tantamount to saying he believed she somehow knew things that other people did not, and he hadn't been ready to do that.

She surprised him then by smiling, though faintly. "You still think I'm a nut. And maybe you're right. But I wish you *would* look into it."

Actually, the more he got to know her, the less he thought of her as a nut. Which didn't mean he accepted everything she said, of course, but he was beginning to acknowledge privately that there were things about Aislinn that weren't easily explained.

She rinsed out their bowls and stacked them in the dishwasher. He stood and picked up the sketch pad, examining the drawing again. Kyle had been little more than a baby when he was lost in that storm, and Ethan's memories of him were hazy, to say the least. But he had looked at enough photos of his little brother to believe that this could be the man he would have become. This drawing resembled quite a bit photos of their father at that age, actually.

"Do you mind if I take this?"

Glancing over her shoulder, she shook her head. "You're welcome to it."

"Thanks." He tore the page neatly from the pad, folded it and slipped it into his shirt pocket. "I'll let you know if I find any evidence at all that either Carmen or Kyle survived that flood."

"Thank you."

She walked him to the front door. He looked around a bit more on the way through the house this time. Her home was tidy, as he had expected, but he was a bit surprised by the lack of color. Shades of brown and cream. Relaxing, he supposed, but it lacked a certain…spark. Passion.

Come to think of it, she tended to dress much the same way, he thought, glancing at her jeans and navy T-shirt. Somewhat colorless. Subdued. With the exception of the flame-red dress Nic had chosen for Aislinn's bridesmaid dress, he couldn't remember ever seeing her wearing bright or bold colors. Another sign of her determination to fit in? Not to call attention to herself, outside of the spectacular cakes that took so much of her time and effort?

They reached for the doorknob at the same time, his hand landing on top of hers. He should have removed his immediately, but instead he lingered, intrigued by the feel of her. She glanced up at him, their eyes meeting. Holding.

She really did have amazing eyes. So dark and deep he could almost fall into them. And her lips. Full. Curvy. Just slightly parted in an invitation he doubted was intentional. Her flawless skin was fair in contrast with her dark hair and eyes, a slight wash of color warming her cheeks as he studied her. He could easily imagine how soft it would feel against his palm.

From the first moment he had seen her, he had been aware of her beauty. He had pushed the attraction to the back of his mind as he had tried to deal with his wariness of everything else about her.

She didn't go pale in response to his touch this time. Instead, her cheeks turned pinker. He wondered what visions, if any, were going through her head this time. He certainly had a few of his own—not that there was anything at all otherworldly about them.

Because those images were becoming just a bit too vivid, he removed his hand slowly,

letting her open the door for him. S̲ urned
the knob, then stepped back to allo̲ n to
pass through the open doorway.

His intention was to walk to his ca̲ out
looking back. Her voice stopped him he
stepped off the front porch. "Ethan?"

He glanced over his shoulder. "Yes

"Be careful at the stoplight."

"What stoplight?"

"Every stoplight," she answered an
the door.

Shaking his head, he climbed into
Seemed like every time he managed t
the more troubling things about her, sh
a way to remind him. Be careful at sto
What sort of psychic advice was that?
that sort of a "duh" admonition?

And yet he found himself hesitating
the light turned green, long enough for th
in the pickup truck behind him to blow his
impatiently. Shaking his head at his own
libility, he started to accelerate—then slamn

on brakes when a teenager in a wannabe
s car squealed through the intersection,
n slowing for the red light.

Ethan not waited, the kid would have
sided him. As it was, he came within an
f being rear-ended by the pickup, which
noved forward when he did.

awing a deep breath to steady his pulse, he
eeded on with caution. There were defi-
ly things about Aislinn that were getting
der all the time to explain, he thought
mly.

Chapter Seven

Even as he dialed his parents' phone number Wednesday evening, Ethan wondered what he was doing. Was he really starting an investigation into his brother's death? All because Aislinn had a feeling Kyle was still alive?

Remembering the incident with the traffic light, he glanced at the drawing that lay beside him. So maybe it was worth asking a few questions. "Mom? Hi, it's me."

"Ethan. Hi, sweetie, how are things there?"

"Okay. We installed some new software on

Joel's computers today. Should simplify his bookkeeping quite a bit."

"Oh, that's nice. Are you almost finished with his new business plan?"

"Yeah. I think he'll see a jump in profits within the next few months."

"You didn't increase his prices, did you, Ethan? Because you know, he takes care of a lot of children whose families don't have a great deal of money."

"I'm not advising him to gouge his patients, Mom. Nor their insurance companies. I've simply found places where he and his partner and staff could cut overhead and minimize waste."

"Oh. That's good then."

He smiled faintly. "Yeah. That's good."

Shifting into a more comfortable position in his brother's easy chair, he cleared his throat. "Mom, do you mind if I ask you a couple of questions about Kyle's accident?"

After a slight pause, she replied, "No, of course not. But what made you think of that tonight?"

He had no intention of mentioning Aislinn, of course. Instead he said, "I guess it's just been on my mind for the past few days. It's been thirty years next month, hasn't it?"

"Yes." She obviously hadn't needed the reminder of the sad anniversary. "What do you want to ask, sweetie?"

He'd made a few notes. He glanced at them, though he didn't want to sound too prepared to his mother. "The nanny—Carmen Nichols, right?"

"Yes. You should have some memories of her. She was with us from the time Kyle was only six months old. That's when I went back to my volunteering and charity work after his birth."

Ethan knew his mother still struggled with guilt that she hadn't been home with Kyle that day. Though she had never worked out of the home full-time after having children, she had been extremely active in local schools and charities, spending part of almost every day volunteering and organizing fund-raisers and other events. It had been almost a year after Kyle's death before she had been able to start volunteering again, and then only during the hours when he and Joel had been safely in school.

As much as he hated bringing those bad memories back to her, he pressed on carefully. "She was nice. Sort of quiet, from what I recall. I remember that she was particularly close to Kyle."

"She adored him. Of course, she was with him more than she was with you and Joel. You were both old enough to be more self-sufficient when she joined us and you were involved in activities of your own before long—preschool and playdates, teeny-league sports activities, that sort of thing."

"How old was Carmen, anyway? I thought of her as being pretty old, but to a little kid, anyone over sixteen is old."

"She was just shy of thirty. She was only a couple of years younger than I was, actually."

"Older than the average nanny."

"A bit. But I'm afraid she wasn't trained to do much else. She told me that she dropped out of high school during her junior year to get married to a young man in the Army. A few years later, he was killed in a rather sordid incident overseas—a bar fight or something— leaving poor Carmen with little means of support. She was estranged from her family, who hadn't approved of the choices she had made, and she was pretty much on her own."

"How did you meet her? Did she apply for the job?"

"Not exactly. I hadn't quite decided whether to hire a nanny, but one of my friends sug- gested that I should meet Carmen. Carmen was working part-time for a day care center where my friend sometimes left her children, and my friend Angela was very impressed with her. She recommended her to me, and your father and I met with her and decided to give it a try. She was wonderful with Kyle, and you and

Joel liked her, so it all worked out nicely. We never regretted hiring her. Even after…"

Her voice faded, but Ethan was able to fill in the rest of the sentence. "So she just became a part of the family? Didn't have an outside life of her own? No boyfriends?"

"No. She had a couple of friends around town but no one particularly close to her. I used to try to talk her into going out more, getting a life outside of our house, but she was too shy. She said she was happy with the way things were and she made it clear that she didn't want me to interfere, so I stopped trying. I always assumed she was still grieving over her husband and that she would decide in her own time when she was ready to move on."

"She didn't live with us, did she?"

"No, she had a little apartment not far away. Ethan, these are very odd questions. It isn't that I mind answering them, but what has made you so curious about Carmen?"

"Just working out some old memories in my

mind," he prevaricated. "Do you mind answering a couple more questions, even if they sound a little strange to you?"

"All right. If it will help you."

"It will." At least he hoped so. "Do you know Carmen's maiden name? And where she grew up?"

"Her maiden name was Smith, I think. And I believe she once told me that she came from Florida. I'm not sure how she ended up in North Carolina, where we lived."

"Does the name Mark mean anything to you?"

"Mark?" She thought a moment, and then he could almost hear her shrug as she replied, "Not particularly. There's a Mark who works in the post office I use. I know because it's printed on his uniform shirt. And Mark Campbell, who goes to the same church your father and I attend. You know him, Ethan. He sells insurance."

"Yeah, I know him." But he doubted that the balding, avuncular insurance salesman had anything to do with Aislinn's premonition. His family hadn't even moved to Alabama until several years after Kyle's disappearance.

There had been a time when he would have thought of it as Kyle's death, he realized abruptly. Was he really letting Aislinn affect his thinking this much? Maybe he was if he was willing to put his mother through what had to be a difficult inquisition. And it was about to get harder for her.

"Why do you ask about the name Mark?"

He shook his head even though she couldn't see him. "Just a name I thought I remembered."

It was the first outright lie he had given her about this, and he didn't like the way it tasted on his tongue. He moved on quickly. "I seem to remember being told that no one knew exactly where Carmen was taking Kyle that afternoon. Is that correct?"

After a moment of silence Elaine replied, "Yes, that's right. As far as anyone knew, there was no reason for her to have left the house with him that day. She rarely took him out, except to the park, occasionally, and the weather was much too bad for that on that day. He didn't have any doctor's appointments, and as far as we could determine, she had no appointments, either. If there had been an emergency of some sort, we'd have expected her to try to reach someone, but we couldn't find any evidence that she'd tried to call anyone."

"Strange."

"Yes. After obsessing about it for a long time, I decided she must have needed something from the store or some other sort of errand, though she drove much farther than she should have had to. There were plenty of stores and shops closer to our house than where her car was found."

"There were no witnesses to the accident?"

"No one who was willing to stay around to talk about it, anyway."

"What does that mean?"

"Don't you remember us talking about it?

Well, maybe you wouldn't. Your father and I tried not to discuss the accident much when you and Joel were young. Anyway, there was an anonymous report. A woman called in the details of where Carmen's car had gone off the road, but she didn't give her name. By the time the police arrived, no one was there, though they found evidence that a car had gone into the river."

"How did they know it was Carmen's car even before they found it?"

"The woman gave a license plate number. She said she caught a glimpse of it just as the car went over. The police seemed to think she might have somehow caused the accident. Maybe skidded or crossed the center line into Carmen's path, and didn't want to admit it. She panicked, apparently."

"Yet she had the presence of mind to note the license plate number?"

"Some people just notice things like that, I guess." She sounded a little weary now, as if this conversation was taking a toll on her.

"Anyway, the police found the car a couple of days later, some distance downriver. Very deep. As you know, they never found Carmen or Kyle. It was months later before they recovered the poor old man who was swept into the river in another part of the state the day earlier, when he got out of his flooded car in chest-deep water. Everyone said it was the worst flooding of the past fifty years.

"That's what made it even harder to imagine why Carmen would have risked taking Kyle out that day," she added. "Everyone knew how bad the flooding problem was. The earlier drownings had been all over the news. It just didn't make sense. It still doesn't after all these years. I've just finally had to accept that we'll never know the answers."

Something he should be telling himself, rather than following the suggestions of a pseudopsychic, Ethan reminded himself grimly. "That's all I wanted to ask, Mom," he said somewhat abruptly. "Thanks for being so patient, okay? I hope it wasn't too distressing for you."

"Of course not, Ethan. I'm always available if you need to talk, you know that."

Feeling decidedly guilty now, he said, "Thanks, Mom. But you've answered all my questions. I'll let you go now. I'm sure you have things to do."

"Actually, I do have a book club meeting this evening. But if you'd rather talk…"

"No. Go to your meeting. And tell Dad hi for me, okay? I'll see you both next week."

"All right. Good night, Ethan."

Feeling like a jerk, he hung up the phone. He wished he could say that conversation had managed to convince him that everything Aislinn had said was a load of bunk. Unfortunately it had only served to remind him that there were still a great many unanswered questions about the events of that long-ago afternoon.

While he wasn't prepared to admit that Aislinn had provided any of those explanations, he knew his mind wouldn't be at ease until he'd made an attempt to pursue a few more answers on his own.

"You haven't been cooperating with the staff, Cassandra. That isn't like you."

She shook her head, speaking patiently. "It isn't the way you make it sound, Dr. Thomas. I'm not exactly refusing to cooperate. I've simply chosen not to take the sleep medications anymore. They don't help, and I don't like the way they make me feel the next day."

"Then let's try another prescription. There are several we haven't tried yet. As you know, everyone reacts differently to medication, and there's a good chance the next one won't cause the aftereffects you don't like. You need your rest. It's obvious that your health is being affected."

She didn't bother to argue with him on that point. She had been feeling weary. Lethargic. Too weak at times to lift her knitting needles.

She never complained, but apparently the staff had been watching her a bit more closely than she had realized—and reporting their observations to her doctor. "I'll be fine."

He frowned, and she could see genuine concern in his pretty green eyes. "I worry about you, Cassandra."

"Do you?" She smiled at him. "That's very sweet, Dr. Thomas."

"It's also my job."

Reaching out, she patted his arm in a maternal gesture. "But it's more than that to you. You worry too much about us. Remember what I warned you about burnout."

"We aren't talking about me," he reminded her, though he couldn't seem to help smiling back at her. "We were discussing you. You aren't sleeping. You're refusing your medications. And you haven't been talking with your counselor. According to her, you're always pleasant and polite but not at all forthcoming about anything that might be bothering you."

"I prefer to keep my problems to myself. Do you have any plans for the weekend, Dr. Thomas?"

Sighing impatiently, he shook a finger at her. "You're trying to change the subject again. Why won't you talk with your counselor? Don't you like her?"

"She's nice enough. A little too perky. I prefer people with a little pepper to them. Like you."

He chuckled. "Flirting with me won't make me forget what we're talking about."

She laughed softly. "Maybe not now. But there was a time when I could have smiled at you and made you forget your name."

"I have no doubt of that."

"My late husband said I mesmerized him the first time he met me. Little did he know I planned it exactly that way."

"Set your cap for him, did you?"

She nodded, remembering her certainty that marrying Lawrence would be vital to her future. Turned out she had been right. Had he not left her so well provided for, who knew where she would be now? "He never knew what hit him."

The young doctor laughed again, though Cassandra hadn't actually been joking. And then he sobered. "You and your husband had no children?"

She shook her head. "I was almost fifty when we married. He was seventy-five and had outlived a wife and a son. I made him very happy for the last few years of his life."

"And did he make you happy?"

She suspected that her smile looked rather sad to him, though she tried to keep her emotions hidden. "He was very kind to me."

After a moment the doctor spoke again. "Forgive me if you think I'm prying, but I've noticed you never have visitors. You have no family?"

"None that I would have any interest in seeing. Or vice versa."

That seemed to surprise him. "I can't imagine anyone not wanting to spend time with you."

"Yes, well, you haven't known me very long. I haven't always been the charming and gracious lady you see now."

He looked at her as though he wasn't quite sure if she was teasing him. She had spoken the truth, of course.

"Still," he said, and something about the way he watched her told her that he was choosing his words very deliberately, "it's a shame you never had children. You wouldn't be so lonely now."

Did he think that was what was bothering her? Loneliness?

Perhaps he was right in a way, she conceded. But she had no intention of telling him everything. "Not everyone is meant to be a mother, Dr. Thomas," she said gently, even as the memory of a baby's cries echoed hauntingly through her mind.

"Maybe not," he said, standing, as if sensing that he'd gotten all he was going to get out of her this time. He paused for a moment beside her chair, setting a gentle hand on her shoulder. "I'd like to try another sleep aid for you, Cassandra. If this one doesn't help you, then perhaps we should pursue some different avenues. Are you willing to work with me?"

Because the poor man looked so genuinely distressed, so anxious to help, she nodded.

"I'll try the new sleep aid," she said. "Maybe this one will work."

He seemed relieved that she had agreed to let him try again to help her. He wanted so badly to be of assistance to her.

His kind nature was going to be severely tested someday, his tender heart broken. That wasn't a guess. It was a certainty. But because she wasn't ready to talk to him about such things, she kept her thoughts to herself.

She waved him out with a smile that faded the moment the door closed behind him.

Ethan left the clinic early Thursday afternoon, but rather than heading back to Joel's house, he drove to Aislinn's shop. She would probably be busy, but he had an urge to stop by anyway. He didn't pause to ask himself why.

She *was* busy, as it turned out. She was meeting with a giggling young woman and her mother, who were trying to decide on a wedding cake design. Sitting at the reception area table with her clients, Aislinn glanced up when Ethan walked in, excused herself and walked over to greet him, leaving the women to leaf slowly through the photo albums of cakes she had previously designed.

"Hi."

He nodded. "Sorry, I didn't mean to interrupt your meeting."

"No problem. I have fresh coffee in the kitchen if you'd like to have a cup while I finish up here."

"Sounds good. Thanks."

"There's cake, too," she added with a smile. "Cupcakes, actually. In the fridge. Help yourself."

"I'll do that."

Leaving her to her customers, he walked back into the kitchen. She had been busy that day, he noted immediately. There were not one but two cakes on the work island.

The largest was obviously a wedding cake, though a bit different than the usual tiers-on-pillars design. This one was stacked in four graduated layers covered in a shiny, almost pearlescent frosting tinted a pale lavender. Amazingly realistic flowers in graduated shades of purple were arranged on the top layer and cascaded down both sides, intertwined with glossy green leaves that he could almost have believed were real had he not looked more closely. Rather than a bride and groom, a delicate white cage sat in the very center of the top, holding two white doves and decorated with thin, purple satin ribbon.

The second cake was more whimsical. A groom's cake, maybe? It looked amazingly like a fisherman's creel with a fly-fishing reel lying on top. Fascinated, he studied the woven effect of the piped frosting, making it look exactly like a natural rattan basket. The top was brown and actually had a wood-grain pattern to it, and the hinges and clasp could well have been made of metal, though he knew they were edible. The reel was made of a small, round layer, decorated so realistically he could almost hear the line zing through it.

Amazing. He couldn't help but wonder if Aislinn was wasting her talents here. It wasn't as if she had family holding her in this area. Not that he could tell, anyway. With the exception of a few close friends and her thriving business, she seemed to live a very solitary life. He'd gotten the impression that she loved her rather colorless home but rarely shared it with anyone else.

Because that seemed all too familiar to him, he winced. He was often called a loner. He, too, kept his somewhat isolated home as a retreat from the demands of the outside world. Nic had once remarked that he and Aislinn were alike in some ways, and he had immediately denied that they had anything at all in common. He didn't want to start rethinking that denial just now.

He poured himself a cup of coffee and opened the refrigerator. The cupcakes were stacked on a plate, arranged almost like a cake themselves. Cheerfully decorated with yellow frosting and pink flowers, they were sort of sissy but looked too good to resist. He plucked one from the top of the stack and carried it and his coffee to the table to wait for Aislinn.

From where he sat, he could easily overhear the conference going on in the other room. He made no effort not to eavesdrop. This was business, after all. His specialty.

He could hear papers rustling as Aislinn began to talk. Probably taking notes. "So your colors are pumpkin and chocolate, is that right? Interesting choices, and very nice for a late fall wedding."

The bride spoke warmly. "Thank you. My fiancé keeps saying I've picked brown and orange and he thinks those are weird colors for a wedding, but I told him pumpkin and chocolate aren't just brown and orange."

"No, of course not," Aislinn agreed.

Bull, Ethan thought. He agreed with the absent fiancé. Call the colors what you wanted, they were still brown and orange. And they did seem like sort of weird colors for a wedding.

Aislinn spoke again. "Have you seen a cake you like in the photo albums? Or do you have ideas for a design you would like me to create for you?"

"Since our wedding will take place in October and the colors are fall colors, I thought maybe something that fit the season, you know? Like maybe leaves and gourds and pumpkins and stuff."

For the first time, the mother of the bride spoke up. "Really, Lacey? Wouldn't you rather have flowers and scallops and more delicate-looking things on your wedding cake?"

"No, Mom. I told you—I want my wedding

to be different. I don't want the same stuff everyone else has."

For the next twenty minutes they debated traditional versus creative wedding rituals while Aislinn contributed an occasional calming suggestion. At times, the discussion between mother and daughter grew rather heated, and Ethan suspected that there had been other such arguments during various stages of the wedding planning. But Aislinn seemed to be an old pro at keeping such conflicts under control, and by the time the duo left a short while later, they seemed to be satisfied with the results of the meeting.

Despite how calm she had sounded, Aislinn looked a bit stressed when she joined Ethan in the kitchen. She headed straight for the coffeepot.

"The wedding isn't until October and they're already ordering the cake?" Ethan asked, watching her.

"I prefer six months' notice," she replied with

a shrug. "They're actually running a little behind. But I think I can work them in, since the cake she wants doesn't sound overly complicated."

"You're booked six months ahead?"

"Yes. I can usually work in a few birthday and special-occasion cakes, but when it comes to the very complicated and labor-intensive cakes, I need lots of notice."

"Do you charge by the hour?"

"By the serving," she corrected. "The price per serving depends on the time involved and the cost of the supplies required."

"Makes sense."

She carried her coffee to the table and slid into the chair opposite him. "Did you have a cupcake?"

"Actually, I had two of them. They were good. What was that filling? Sort of lemony?"

"A lemon-orange flavor. A new recipe I'm trying."

"I'd add it to the menu."

"Thanks. I'll take your advice into consideration."

"I usually get paid for my advice."

"And I usually get paid for my cupcakes."

He chuckled. "We'll call it even."

They smiled at each other across the table, and he was rather surprised by how friendly and relaxed they were being with each other. Usually there was an undercurrent of tension, if not open antagonism, between them—and he was well aware that it was mostly his fault. He didn't know exactly what had changed in his attitude toward her—heck, he didn't even know why he was with her now, but it felt kind of nice.

Maybe that was what spurred him to tell her, "I talked to my mother yesterday."

She looked at him over the rim of her coffee cup, waiting for him to continue.

"I asked her some questions about Kyle's accident."

"That must have been a difficult conversation for both of you."

Major understatement. "Yeah. It was."

"Did you tell her about me?"

"No. I just implied that the subject was on my mind because the thirtieth anniversary of Kyle's death is coming up soon."

Aislinn didn't bother to remind him that she didn't believe Kyle was dead. Instead, she asked, "Did you learn anything new from your mother?"

He repeated the conversation as best he could remember, and she sat quietly listening and drinking her coffee.

"The authorities looked for Kyle and Carmen for weeks before giving up," he added. "They said they could have been carried miles away from the place they went in, considering how fast and how high the river was that week."

She remained silent.

Looking at her narrowly, he asked, "I don't suppose you can give me any other details about what happened that afternoon?"

Frowning a little, she seemed to look inward, as if searching her mind for the answer to his question. But then she shook her head. "All I know is that they didn't die that day."

"That day?"

"Kyle is still living. I don't know whether Carmen is alive."

He stood and poured himself another cup of coffee. "This gift of yours," he said, annoyed at his own awkwardness, "have you ever used it to—you know—like, help Nic or something?"

"I don't—"

"I guess I'm trying to ask if you've ever worked with the police to find missing persons. Anything like that."

She frowned. "Of course not. I couldn't do anything like that."

"Don't you ever get feelings about the cases Nic works?"

"Sometimes, but I rarely say anything to her about it. I wouldn't want to mislead her in any way. I make guesses, Ethan, and they aren't always right."

"So how often are you wrong?"

"I don't keep records."

This time he was the one who remained silent, looking at her steadily across the table.

She sighed. "When I get a certain type of strong feeling, I'm almost always right. But I rarely have clear enough details to help the police or anything like that. For example, I had a premonition that Nic was going to be injured in an accident last year in Alabama—but I didn't have a clue how or when it was going to happen. I couldn't prevent her from being hurt. So what good was it, really?"

He twisted his coffee cup between his hands, thinking of how frustrating that would have been. To know her friend would be hurt yet not be able to prevent it.

"It's the same with you," she added. "I know your brother is alive, but I can't tell you where he is. Where he has been for the past thirty years. What happened on that long-ago afternoon. So you tell me—just how useful is this so-called gift of mine?"

Ethan didn't know quite how to respond to her plaintive question. Yet he was struck by the sincerity of her expression. The visible distress in her eyes. If she was faking, she was perhaps the best actor he had ever encountered.

"You kept me from being broadsided at a traffic light," he offered, compelled for some reason to try to encourage her.

"Did I?"

He nodded. "You didn't provide specifics, but I kept your advice in mind. Maybe that's what makes it useful. You give warnings, but it's up to the people you tell to figure out how take advantage of them."

"Does that mean you're starting to believe I'm not just making up the things I tell you?"

Had he just been cleverly manipulated? He frowned, searching her expression again for any subtle sign of satisfaction. Seeing nothing, he shrugged, saying noncommittally, "Let's just say I'm keeping an open mind."

"That's something, anyway," she said.

"Best I can do." He stood, carrying his coffee cup to the sink. "Are you about done here for the day? If so, you want to go have dinner somewhere?"

"Dinner?" She seemed as surprised by the invitation as he was that he had impulsively issued it. "Now?"

"Whenever you're ready." After all, he reasoned, he was tired of eating alone. And at least Aislinn was good company who wouldn't read anything more than he intended into the outing. Heck, she would probably know how the evening would end before he did.

She studied him a moment from her chair, as if trying to determine his motive for asking—and then she nodded and stood. "All right. I can clear up here in about ten minutes, if you don't mind waiting."

"Not at all."

He wandered into the reception area to leaf through albums of her work while she prepared to leave. He noted there wasn't one wedding cake with pumpkins on it. Yet he had no doubt that if Aislinn designed one, it would look good. When it came to her business, he had complete faith in her abilities.

Chapter Eight

She wouldn't exactly say she was winning Ethan over, but at least he didn't seem openly antagonistic anymore. She supposed that was a step forward.

Not that she was trying to win him over, exactly, Aislinn assured herself as she sliced into a steak at the restaurant where she and Ethan had decided to dine. He would be leaving town in a few days, after all. She just didn't like the thought of him leaving while still thinking of her as a con artist or a crazy person.

Maybe he was finally starting to see that she was just an average woman with above-average intuition.

Even with his self-proclaimed ineptitude at small talk, Ethan managed to carry on a civil conversation with her as they ate. They didn't talk about anything of particular importance. Mostly business stuff—his and her own. If there was one thing that got Ethan excited, she thought with a secret smile, it was business.

"Aislinn." Pamela Maclure stopped by the table, looking delighted to see her. Her round, reddish-toned face beamed with the smile she turned from Aislinn to Ethan. "It's great to see you. And you're Joel Brannon's brother, aren't you? I saw you at the wedding."

"Ethan Brannon," he confirmed with a nod, rising to greet her.

Looking pleased with the small courtesy, she extended her hand. "I'm Pamela Maclure. An old friend of Aislinn's."

"Nice to meet you."

"You, too. Please, sit down. I only stopped by to say hello."

Ethan returned to his seat and picked up his fork again.

Pamela turned back to Aislinn. "Look, call me tomorrow, okay? I need to talk to you about something."

Aislinn groaned, knowing exactly what Pamela wanted to talk to her about. "Not another one, Pam. I'm really not interested, okay?"

Pamela frowned and glanced quickly at Ethan. "No, really, this might really work out. Unless you're, um—"

"No," she said firmly, shaking her head. She and Ethan were definitely not an item, which was what Pamela had implicitly asked. "Still not interested."

Happily married Pamela had been trying for months to fix her up with a string of men, none of whom had been in the least compatible with her. It didn't help that Pamela billed Aislinn as her friend the psychic, which intrigued some men for all the wrong reasons. She would rather spend an evening with Ethan, who openly expressed his skepticism of such abilities, than with a guy who hoped to profit from them, as had the man who'd offered to split the take with her if she would help him place bets on winning football teams.

Pamela sighed. "This is what I get for being friends with someone who knows what I'm planning," she muttered, only half-teasingly. "I can't get anything past you."

Aislinn gave her a warning look.

Sighing again, more gustily this time, Pamela took a step backward. "Call me anyway," she said. "Just to talk."

"I will," Aislinn promised. And she would, because despite everything, she was fond of Pamela.

Smiling at Ethan again, Pamela excused herself and went to rejoin her husband, who had just finished paying at the cash register.

"What was that about?" Ethan asked quizzically.

She lifted a shoulder. "Long story."

He didn't push. "You say you've known her a long time?"

"Yes. Since high school. She's a good friend."

"Does she know about your...well, you know?"

Resisting the impulse to roll her eyes, Aislinn said shortly, "She knows."

"Have you ever had a feeling that helped her out?"

"A few times."

"And she believed you. Took your advice to heart."

She nodded. "Of course."

"Can you give me an example?"

She lifted her eyebrows at him.

"Hey, you're expecting me to go to a lot of trouble to pursue one of your hunches. It wouldn't hurt to give me some verification that I wouldn't be wasting my time."

"You're asking for references?"

His mouth twitched. "Just anecdotal evidence."

"Fine." She propped her elbows on the table and loosely clasped her hands. "I told her where to find her husband."

"Had she lost him?"

"Not like that. I told her where to go to meet him initially. I had a feeling she should go to a certain store at a certain time, and she did—and as she was driving through the parking lot, looking for an open space, someone backed into her car."

Ethan lifted an eyebrow. "And that was a good thing?"

"Yes. Bill, her husband, was driving the car that hit hers. He apologized, they exchanged insurance information—and phone numbers—and a year later they were married."

"And you knew she was going to meet him that way."

"Oh, no. I just knew she should be at that

place at that time. I wasn't sure why, but I felt like it was important."

"And now she's trying to repay the favor."

"I beg your pardon?"

He smiled briefly. "It was obvious that she's trying to set you up. With someone you're not interested in meeting, apparently."

Aislinn sighed, wondering if she was the only one at this table with better-than-average intuition. "I don't know who she's picked out for me this time, but you're right. She's undoubtedly got another prospect in mind."

"Another prospect?"

"She's been trying to match me up for more than a year. She's made it her personal mission."

"Actually, she reminds me of someone. My dad has this office manager—Heidi Rosenbaum. Nice woman, but she can't bear to see a single adult. She's always trying to match people up. I ran into her at the grocery store last month and she started telling me about some woman she wanted me to meet. A schoolteacher."

"And you told her you weren't interested."

"I told her I was fully capable of finding my own dates if I wanted."

"Why do I get the feeling you weren't particularly polite about it?" she asked, amused by the image.

"Let's just say subtlety doesn't work well with Heidi."

"Did you hurt her feelings?"

"Not possible. She just patted my arm and told me I knew where to find her if I got too lonely."

She studied his face. She doubted that he had much trouble finding companionship when he wanted it. But she suspected that for the most part he was content with his own company.

"You don't get lonely very often."

"Right."

"But you get sad sometimes."

He frowned. "I don't know what you're talking about."

He knew. But he didn't want to talk about it.

And she wouldn't press just now, while they were getting along so well.

Ethan changed the subject rather abruptly. "How are you with a computer?"

"In what respect?"

"I thought I'd go online on Joel's computer this evening, maybe do a little research about Carmen Nichols. Needless to say, I don't have a lot of experience with that sort of investigation. I just wondered if you have any advice to offer."

"I haven't had any experience at finding long-lost people, either," she replied. "But I spend a lot of time online looking for inspiration for new cake designs, learning new methods, that sort of thing."

"Maybe between the two of us, we could find some information—if you're not too busy and you're interested in looking into it with me, of course."

"You're asking me to come to Joel's this evening and help you do computer research?" she asked for clarification.

He nodded. "Unless you have other plans."

He had taken her by surprise again—just as he had when he'd shown up at her shop and when he'd asked her to dinner. Why was Ethan suddenly looking for ways to spend time with her?

"I don't have other plans, actually," she admitted. "But I don't know how much help I would be to you."

He shrugged. "It was just a thought."

Maybe he was just trying to make amends, of sorts, for the way he had treated her from the time they'd met. Maybe he figured that since she was his new sister-in-law's best friend, it was better to stay on friendly footing. Or maybe, despite his denials, he was just getting a little lonely after all, here in this town where he knew so few people.

"All right," she said, hoping she wasn't making a mistake. "Maybe together we can find some information that would lead you to your brother."

While he looked far from convinced that their search would change his mind about what had happened to Kyle all those years ago, he seemed satisfied that she had agreed to assist him.

Aislinn followed Ethan to Joel's house after dinner. She stopped by to say hello to Nic's mother next door before joining Ethan. Susan seemed to be enjoying her visit home, but she admitted to Aislinn that she was looking forward to returning to Europe to be with her son. She would spend another couple of weeks here after Nic and Joel returned, visiting with them, and then she would return to Paris until her next visit home at Thanksgiving.

Susan didn't seem to find it odd that Aislinn was visiting Ethan that evening. She seemed to believe that Aislinn was simply being sociable, keeping her friend's brother company for a few hours. Aislinn was content to leave it at that. Taking her leave of Susan after a brief, pleasant exchange, she walked back to Joel's house to help Ethan search for his long-lost brother.

* * *

Curled into a chair next to Ethan's, Aislinn arched her back and was rather surprised when several muscles protested. She glanced at her watch. Had they really been sitting here for almost two hours, staring at Joel's computer monitor?

Ethan sat in another chair at the keyboard, a legal pad with several pages of scribbled notes at his elbow. He looked around when Aislinn moved. "Getting tired?"

"Just a little stiff." She stood, stretching out the kinks. "Do you mind if I have a glass of water?"

"Of course not. There's a filtered pitcher in the refrigerator. Help yourself."

"Thank you. Can I get you a glass?"

"Yeah, that sounds good. Thanks."

She was returning with a glass in each hand when the telephone rang. "That's Joel," she said without checking caller ID. "I assume you're not going to tell him yet what we're doing."

"You assume correctly." He answered the phone, chatting for a few minutes with his brother while Aislinn sipped her water.

She was beginning to think he wasn't going to mention her at all when she heard him ask if Nic was nearby. "Aislinn's here, keeping me company for a while," he added. "They'd probably like to say hello to each other."

Taking the receiver from him with a smile, Aislinn said, "Hi, Nic. How's the honeymoon?"

"Paradise," Nic answered fervently. "It's so beautiful here, you wouldn't believe it. It's going to be tough coming back home and going back to work. And speaking of home, how's everything there?"

"Same as always. I saw your mom earlier. She's having a great time catching up with her old friends."

"I talked to her yesterday. It did seem like she was enjoying her visit. I could tell she's looking forward to rejoining Paul, though. She really loves it over there." Changing the subject, Nic continued, "So, you're spending the evening with Ethan."

"Yes, we've been having a nice visit."

"Have you?" Nic sounded surprised—and a bit suspicious, as if she wondered what exactly was going on between Aislinn and Ethan.

Aislinn didn't blame her for being curious. After all, neither she nor Ethan were overly sociable types. And they hadn't exactly gotten off to the best start.

"Has Ethan been giving you advice about your business? Joel said there's nothing he loves to do more than talk to small-business owners about ways they can restructure."

"Yes, he's given me a few tips about my business." He had advised her to add the choco-late-caramel cake and the lemon-orange cupcakes to her menu, which she supposed made her answer an honest one.

Looking around from the computer, Ethan gave her a quizzical look. She wrinkled her nose at him and returned her attention to the phone call.

"I'd better go," Nic said. "Joel and I are going for a late-night walk on the beach."

"Sounds very romantic."

"I guess it would be if one of us didn't insist on starting a footrace every time."

Aislinn laughed. "Gee, I wonder which one of you that would be."

They hung up shortly afterward.

"I appreciate you not telling them what you and I are really working on this evening," Ethan said without looking around again.

She returned to her seat beside him. "I promised you I wouldn't."

"Do you always know who's calling before you pick up the phone?"

"It was a pretty safe guess that would be Joel."

"True, but you didn't answer my question."

She sighed. "I usually know, especially on my home phone."

"How often? On your home phone."

"Maybe nine out of ten calls."

"That's a little more than random chance."

"Maybe."

To her relief, he let it go. "I don't think we're going to find anything else tonight, do you?"

"No." She was sure they wouldn't, actually. She'd known for the past half hour that there was nothing left to find online, but she'd kept quiet, letting Ethan check every possibility he could think of.

Pushing away from the desk, he turned his chair to face hers, the legal pad in his hand. "So we've read every old news report we can find of the storm and the accident. We've learned that a couple of people expressed concern at the time that the bodies were never found, but that eventually everyone seemed to accept that the severity of the flood made the search too difficult. Prevailing theories seemed to be that Carmen and Kyle were trapped at the bottom of the river somewhere beneath debris and would never be found."

Aislinn nodded. "That's what most people believed."

"I remember that my dad went out every day for a long time, driving down the river, taking his fishing boat out whenever he could. After the first night, he didn't believe Kyle was still alive, but he hoped to finally find him so they could give him a decent burial."

Her heart twisting at the grief the family must have experienced, Aislinn murmured, "There was nothing for him to find."

"From what I recall, my mother was amazingly strong during the whole ordeal. Later I heard her tell people that she got through it by concentrating on Joel and me. She said she didn't have the luxury of going to pieces because we depended on her so much."

"I could tell your mother is a resilient woman. She's been through a lot."

"She has."

"Was she close to your sister-in-law? Joel's first wife?"

It was probably because she was watching him so closely that she saw the emotions swirl in his eyes. Most people wouldn't have seen them, she guessed. Ethan was very good at hiding his feelings.

"Yes, she and Heather were very close."

"I'm glad she's been able to welcome Nic to your family as warmly as she has. I know it was difficult for her at first."

"Mom never wanted Joel to be alone forever. And it had been six years since Heather died. Nic was just a little different than Mom had expected. Once she got to know her, she couldn't help but like her."

She'd picked up some undercurrents in that exchange that she wanted to mull over later. For now, she directed the topic back to their search. "So now that we've found out all we can online, what are you going to do to find more information about Carmen?"

"I don't know," he admitted. "I'm no private investigator."

"Have you considered hiring one?"

"And tell him what? That a woman who denies being a psychic has a feeling my long-lost brother is still alive and possibly living somewhere in Georgia?"

"It does sound a little far-fetched when you put it that way."

"Yeah. A little."

"But I'm sure private investigators have heard stranger stories."

"Probably. But I'm not sure I'm willing to pay some guy an outrageous hourly fee to look into this."

Especially since he was still a long way from being convinced there was anything to look into, Aislinn finished silently.

"Maybe you should look up some of Carmen's surviving family members. Maybe some of her friends."

"And ask them what? If they've heard from her?"

She shook her head. "They wouldn't have.

But maybe they had noticed odd behavior from her in the days or weeks leading up to the accident. Maybe they heard her talk about places she wanted to visit or things she wished she could do. Anything that might lead you into a new direction."

"Sounds like a lot of trouble," he grumbled.

"It will be," she agreed. "But it's worth a try, isn't it?"

"Is it?" His expression had turned distant and brooding again, to her regret. It had been kind of nice working side by side with him, having him seem open to her input, willing to accept the possibility that there could be some validity to the things she had told him. But something had changed, and it seemed to have happened when she'd mentioned his late sister-in-law.

Clasping her hands in front of her, she leaned slightly forward in her chair, their knees almost touching as they faced each other. "If there's a chance—even a very slim chance—that I'm right about Kyle still being alive, wouldn't you want to find him?"

Ethan was silent for so long that she began to wonder if he was going to respond. And then he lifted one shoulder. "I guess so. I mean, I haven't ever really considered the possibility that he survived that flood. What you're talking about—kidnapping—was never something my family even considered after he disappeared. Yeah, sure, they wondered why Carmen took him out that day in weather like that. They wondered why no bodies were ever found, but considering the circumstances, that wasn't out of the realm of possibilities."

He pushed his chair back and stood, walking across the room to stare out a window. She doubted that he saw anything out in the neatly manicured back lawn. Even though he wasn't looking at her, his attention was focused entirely on her as he said, "Now, thirty years later, you tell me there's a chance Kyle could have survived. That he somehow grew up without us, matured into a stranger with a different history than ours, probably no memory of any of us."

She had already thought of those things—how painful it would be for the family to accept the years they had lost with Kyle, how wrenching it would be for Elaine and Lou, especially. Moving to stand beside him, she spoke quietly. "It's going to be difficult, for all of you."

He turned, glaring at her in a way that might have intimidated some people. "I'm beginning to wonder if we're both crazy. You for the things you say and me for listening to them."

Though she could understand why he would feel that way, she couldn't help flinching in response to his adjective. "Neither one of us is crazy," she said more forcefully than she had intended.

"Then why am I listening to you?"

She gazed up at him. "Because you're keeping an open mind—just in case I'm right."

"I'm not sure that's it."

"Then why *are* you listening to me?"

He surprised her by reaching up to cup her face between his hands. "Maybe it has something to do with your eyes."

"What—" She had to stop to clear her throat. "What about my eyes?"

Looking somberly down at her, he murmured, "They're mesmerizing. Maybe you're really a hypnotist rather than a psychic."

She tried to smile. "Very funny."

His head lowered toward hers. "I don't think I was joking."

His lips were on hers before she had a chance to say anything else.

Chapter Nine

There were no predictions or special insights in Aislinn's mind when Ethan kissed her. Actually, there was nothing at all. He had rendered her completely incapable of forming a coherent thought.

She hadn't kissed many men in her solitary, self-protective life. But she didn't need much of a base of comparison to know that Ethan was pretty much a pro at this. Amazing, actually.

She couldn't imagine why he was kissing

her. And it utterly astonished her to realize that she was kissing him back.

She gaped up at him when he lifted his head. Then, concerned that she probably looked like an idiot, she closed her mouth and jerked away from him.

Ethan spun on one heel and moved back to stare out the window again. He stood straight and stiff, tension vibrating from every inch of him. Was he regretting kissing her? Wondering what on earth had possessed him? She didn't have a clue what he was thinking.

"I suppose you were expecting that," he said after a moment.

"What are you talking about?" Peevishly, she pushed a lock of hair out of her face. "I had no idea."

"You mean you didn't predict it?"

"No," she answered shortly.

"Interesting."

She stared at his back with mounting irritation. "You're *testing* me? Trying to see if I can predict your actions?"

Without looking around, he shrugged.

"What more do you want me to do to convince you that you can trust me?"

"You could always try some more parlor tricks."

Planting her fists on her hips, she drawled, "Want me to read your mind?"

That made him turn toward her. "You can't."

"You're right. I can't. I have no idea what's going on in that head of yours just now."

She thought she saw a brief flash of relief in his eyes, but that couldn't be right, since he didn't believe she had any special abilities anyway. "You want to convince me? Help me find my brother."

"Isn't that what I've been doing tonight?"

"Hardly. We looked up a couple of old reports of the accident. Easy enough to do. For all I know, you'd already done so."

"I told you I hadn't. But that goes back to whether you can trust anything I say, doesn't it?"

He nodded to concede her point. "Help me find some proof that Kyle survived that flood, and I'll be a lot more likely to believe you."

"I wouldn't know how to begin."

"I have a few ideas."

"Such as?"

"You're the one who suggested I contact Carmen's surviving family and friends. Go with me to talk to them."

"Go with you? I thought you would just talk to them by phone."

He shook his head. "This is too complicated to handle by phone. I need to see their expressions if there's any chance that one of them knows anything about that day that hasn't already been revealed."

"Maybe. But why on earth would you want me there with you?"

"You're the one who claims to just know things. Maybe you'd know if anyone tries to hide something from us."

"So I'd be your human lie detector."

"Something like that."

She shook her head. "I really don't think this is a good idea. For one thing, I'm very busy right now."

"I can wait until you aren't busy. It isn't like there's any hurry."

But there was, she thought, chewing on her lower lip. Somehow she knew that he needed to start his search soon or he would never find the answers. "I really see no need for you to take me along."

"Because you know there's very little chance that there's anything for me to find?"

He was trying to trap her, she thought with a glare. To somehow make her admit she wasn't really convinced Kyle was still alive. "You know what I believe."

"So are you willing to back up your words with action?"

"You really are testing me," she said slowly. "Why?"

He seemed to mull over the question for a

moment before replying. "It seems like something I need to do."

It was like him not to try to offer rationalizations. But she could figure out part of his reasoning. He was still concerned about her closeness to Nic—which made her a part of Joel's life, as well. He had an older-brother protectiveness toward Joel. Toward his whole family, for that matter.

He was undoubtedly worried that despite her promises to him, she would say something to Joel or his parents about her belief that Kyle was still alive. It wasn't necessary for him to explain how distressing that would be for them without proof of her claim. It would be hard enough for them when it turned out to be true.

And it wasn't only his family he was worried about, she sensed. There was a tiny part of him that was starting to believe her, and that disturbed him as much as anything.

She knew he had been burned in the past. She

knew he had put his faith in at least one person who had turned out to be untrustworthy. Because of those betrayals, combined with the hard losses his family had known, he had become guarded. Wary. Unwilling to open himself to further disillusionment.

It would be hard for anyone to believe the earthshaking news she had shared with him, she mused. For Ethan, it was almost impossible, based on nothing more than her instincts.

He would never know, of course, how difficult it was for her to accept it herself. He didn't know how hard she had tried to talk herself out of confiding in Ethan, telling herself that he would probably throw her out on her ear, and that even if he gave her the benefit of the doubt, it would be cruel to raise his hopes with so little evidence. And yet she had known that she was right. Believed it with every fiber of her being. And she had been compelled to tell him, feeling that he had a right to know his brother was alive.

He didn't believe her. He didn't trust her. And yet, rather than keeping her at a distance and refusing to listen to her, he had been spending time with her. Trying to figure her out. And even though he saw it as more of an invitation than a dare, in effect, he was giving her a chance to prove herself to him. To help him find the brother she knew was still out there somewhere.

"Have you gone into a trance?"

His sarcastic question brought her attention back to the moment. "I can take off the week after next if you can," she said, and it was as much a challenge as the one he'd thrown at her. He wanted her to prove herself? Fine. She was demanding that he give her a real chance to do so.

For only a moment he looked startled that she'd accepted his dare. Had he been bluffing?

But then he nodded. "I can probably arrange that."

She swallowed, wondering if she'd made a mistake. But she hid her doubts behind a brusque tone. "Fine. We'll need to work out a plan. And a cover story, if you're still opposed to telling your family what we're doing."

"We can do that. You don't have any cakes ordered for that week?"

"Actually, I'd blocked that week out for a vacation," she said, wondering now if she had somehow sensed that she needed to leave some spare time in her calendar.

"And you're willing to spend your vacation helping me track down a ghost?"

"He's not a ghost," she said firmly. "He's as alive as you are."

"Looks like you've got one week to prove that."

"That will be enough."

His eyebrows rose. "Something else you just know?"

She shrugged. "I guess we'll find out, won't we?"

Turning on one heel, she snatched up her

purse as she headed for the door, suddenly needing some distance from him. "I'm heading home. We'll talk later about the details of our search."

"Right." He followed her toward the door.

She opened it before he could reach her, stepping quickly out into the evening air. Her hand was still on the door when she turned to say, "By the way, Ethan—"

He stood just inside the house, watching her make her exit. "Yeah?"

"You didn't kiss me as a test. You kissed me because you wanted to."

He crossed his arms over his chest in what might be interpreted as a defensive posture, though his drawl was meant to sound rather mocking. "Think so, do you?"

"I do." And that was the woman speaking, not the sort-of psychic. "But from now on? Wait for an invitation."

She closed the door with a snap, giving him no chance to respond.

* * *

"So, Cassandra, have you been sleeping better since Dr. Thomas changed your medications?"

"Much better." Whatever name she had used, whatever identity she had assumed, Cassandra had always been a highly skilled liar.

"That's wonderful." Melanie Hunt, the counselor who had been assigned to Cassandra, smiled her cheery smile and made a note in the file she held.

Cassandra had often wondered whimsically if Melanie had found a way to have that smile permanently affixed. Some sort of clever plastic surgery, perhaps. She was pretty sure she could tell the perpetually perky psychologist that she was planning to sneak out of the institution that evening and rob a bank, and Melanie would just smile and nod and make another note in the file. Maybe ask Dr. Thomas to prescribe some new meds.

But that was unkind. And she was trying to

be a better person these days. She was sure Melanie meant well. Hers wasn't an easy job, and she was performing it to the best of her abilities. Which were just a tiny bit limited, that old, less charitable voice whispered.

"What shall we talk about today?" Melanie asked brightly.

Arranging the almost-finished sweater she was knitting more comfortably on her lap, Cassandra started another row. "You're directing this session. Isn't that your call?"

"I'd like to talk about something important to you, Cassandra. Why don't we chat about your childhood?"

The needles stuttered a bit, but she spoke evenly. "It was fine. Quite nice, actually."

She really was a very accomplished liar.

"Would you like to tell me any amusing stories from your youth?"

"Not particularly."

Melanie managed to smile and sigh in exasperation all at the same time, proving she had some impressive talents of her own. "Oh, Cassandra, you are such a hoot."

A hoot. Well, she supposed it was better than some of the names she'd been called in her time.

Someone tapped on the open door. "Is this a bad time?"

Both Cassandra and Melanie smiled then. Cassandra noted that Melanie's smile had a newly flirtatious element to it. Melanie was wasting her time in that respect, she thought as the handsome young doctor strolled into the room. Dr. Thomas wasn't interested. He'd learned his lesson about dating coworkers.

"Dr. Hunt." He greeted her with professional courtesy, then turned to pat Cassandra's shoulder, his tone turning warmer. "How's my favorite patient?"

Even though she suspected he said that to everyone here, she couldn't help but respond, "I'm doing very well, thank you."

His eyes were more perceptive than Melanie's

as he searched her face. This one was a little harder to deceive.

"I was just trying to persuade her to tell me a funny story from her childhood," Melanie chirped. "But she doesn't seem to be in the mood to reminisce."

Cassandra almost told her that she was never in the mood to reminisce. Living in the present had been her philosophy for the past twelve years, since she had married Lawrence and put her past behind her. But she kept those thoughts to herself.

She sensed that the doctor and the psychologist shared a look before Dr. Thomas said, "That sweater is a very intricate pattern, isn't it? You've made quite a bit of progress on it. It looks almost finished."

"Almost." It had taken her quite a while, actually, since she'd never become very fast at knitting and this was the most complicated pattern she had ever tried. But there had been no reason to hurry, after all.

"Are you making it for yourself?"

"Oh, no. It wouldn't fit me."

"Someone special?"

"Mmm."

The doctor laughed ruefully. "You don't give an inch, do you?"

"You know what they say. Give an inch, and they'll take a mile."

Shaking his head, he patted her shoulder again. "Then we'll wait until you're ready to share."

What he didn't add was, *If ever,* though it was implied. That was one thing about this private and very expensive facility. As long as she had the money to stay, she could pretty much cooperate with the staff or not, as she desired. And since she had plenty of money and cooperated just enough not to be a problem for the administration, she wasn't going anywhere.

The headphones covering Aislinn's ears discouraged conversation from the chatty-looking little lady sitting in the seat next to her. It wasn't that Aislinn was trying to be unsociable, exactly. She was simply too nervous to engage in conversation with an overly friendly stranger.

She didn't do well in close quarters, like this airplane cabin. So she sat here, crammed into a window seat, her hands clenched in her lap and soothing music playing in her ears, trying to focus on the melodies and the lyrics.

Unfortunately the music didn't drown out the insights she picked up from all the people crowded around her. The sweet-natured woman next to her wanted to talk about her grandchildren, whom she was on her way to visit. The man in front of her was a salesman wearily embarking on yet another business trip. Someone else was traveling with a woman who was not his wife—and hoping his wife would not find out.

She wasn't reading thoughts. She couldn't add many details to those flashes of information. There was nothing she could do for any of them, though she supposed she could inform the philanderer that his wife would learn about the girlfriend—and that it was going to cost him. Big.

Maybe it was possible that she would learn something she could change. An impending car accident or some other tragedy she could divert with a warning. But that would involve tracking down whomever she'd picked up on, and then convincing that person that she wasn't a nut and that her warnings should be taken seriously. And because she didn't want to be led away in a straitjacket or—equally daunting—believed and then expected to possess more wisdom and guidance, she had no intention of opening herself to more.

She cranked up the music just a little, as if doing so would drown out any extra thoughts in her head. Instead she found herself thinking about an all-new problem. The man who was supposed to be waiting for her when the plane touched down at the airport in North Carolina.

It had been more than a week since she'd last seen Ethan. He'd left Arkansas on Saturday, two days after they'd spent the evening with Joel's computer. They had seen each other only once after that night: he'd stopped by her shop to tell her he was leaving, and to inform her that he would call with details of their trip. Unless she'd changed her mind? She had coolly informed him that of course she hadn't changed her mind and she would look forward to his call.

She had spent the eight days since staying very busy at work and firmly not thinking about kissing Ethan.

She couldn't quite believe she was doing this, joining Ethan in another state on a search for the brother he didn't even believe was still alive. But he had pretty much dared her to prove she wasn't crazy, and she'd been unable to resist the challenge.

Maybe she needed to prove a few things to herself, as well.

Ethan was waiting at the baggage claim, as he had promised he would be. She spotted him almost immediately after turning the corner. Though he wasn't tall enough to tower over the milling crowds and was doing nothing to call attention to himself, her gaze went straight to him.

He leaned against a wall, arms crossed over his chest, his expression inscrutable. More than one passing woman checked him out, some rather lingeringly, but he didn't seem to notice any of them. He simply waited. For her.

Spotting her, he straightened away from the wall and moved toward her. He wore jeans. And wore them well. His shirt was a green polo that fit just tightly enough. He was a man who would look equally masculine and comfortable in a three-piece wool suit as he did in denim and soft knit.

She had hoped the week they'd spent apart

had given her a chance to recover from her initial problematic attraction to him. It hadn't.

Telling herself this was simply a normal reaction to a good-looking man and that there was no reason she couldn't put it aside and concentrate on their mission, she stepped forward to greet him. "Hello, Ethan."

"Did you have a good flight?"

"Yes, it was fine," she replied blandly, seeing no need to embellish.

"I've rented a car. Let's get your bags and get out of here."

She nodded and turned toward the luggage carousel, hoping she looked as blasé about this whole thing as Ethan did.

Chapter Ten

Fifteen minutes later they were on the road in the small but comfortable vehicle Ethan had procured for them. "Did you have any problems clearing your schedule for the trip?" he asked.

"Not too many. My employees can take messages until I get back. How about you?"

"I had to reschedule a few things, but I handled it."

"One of the perks of being self-employed, right?"

"Yeah."

She shifted into a more comfortable position, rearranging the seat belt across her lap. Like Ethan, she had dressed casually for travel. She wore a tan wrapped top over a cream-colored tank, slightly darker brown twills and brown leather flats. She hadn't given a great deal of thought to her outfit, simply choosing pieces that were nonbinding and wrinkle-resistant.

"So what was your cover story to get away? I assume you didn't tell anyone you were joining me here?"

She shook her head, trying not to feel too guilty about the fibs she had left behind her. "I told everyone I'd been working too hard and needed a week to rest. Since that wasn't much of a lie, no one really thought too much about it. Except for Nic, of course."

"And what did you tell her?"

"I just told her I had some things I needed to do and I didn't want to talk about it yet."

"That satisfied her?"

Aislinn smiled a little. "Of course not. But we

respect each other enough to give each other space when we need it. She knows I'll tell her what I want her to know when I'm ready."

When he merely nodded, she asked, "What about you? What did you tell everyone about being out of town this week?"

"I go off on business trips fairly often. No one thinks twice about it. They know they can reach me on my cell phone if they need me."

"Same here." Which reminded her that she hadn't turned her phone back on after getting off the plane. She dug into her canvas-and-leather bag and rectified that right then. Not that she expected any calls for a while.

"I thought we would grab a bite of lunch and then get started," Ethan said a few minutes later.

"Fine."

"You in the mood for anything in particular?"

"No. Anything's okay with me."

Taking her at her word, he turned into the

parking lot of a tidy diner that advertised "country cooking" and appeared to be popular, judging by the number of vehicles in the smallish parking lot. "There should be something here we'll both like," he remarked.

"I'm sure you're right."

A smiling waitress in jeans, T-shirt and apron greeted them at the door and escorted them to what appeared to be the last available table. "What can I get you to drink?"

"Iced tea for me, please," Aislinn replied.

Ethan nodded to second the order, and the busy waitress bustled off to get their drinks, leaving them with menus to peruse until she returned. Aislinn took a moment to look around. It was a little early for the Sunday after-church lunch crowd, but the diner was still full. The other patrons seemed to be enjoying their meals, talking and laughing so that the room was filled with the clatter of tableware and the sounds of camaraderie.

No one seemed particularly interested in her

and Ethan, and for once she was picking up nothing from anyone else that gave her any cause for concern. She could enjoy her lunch and feel as normal as anyone else here.

She looked back across the table to find Ethan studying her over the top of his menu. "What?"

"I was just wondering what was going through your mind when you looked around the room," he answered candidly.

She glanced down at the menu, trying to concentrate on the choices. "I doubt that you would understand," she murmured.

"Try me."

It was almost tempting, just to see how he would react. She was rather relieved when the waitress returned then with their drinks, giving her a chance to change her mind.

"Have y'all decided what you want?"

Aislinn looked quickly down at the menu again and chose the first thing that appealed to her. "I'll have the grilled chicken breast."

"Just bring me the special," Ethan said, handing over his menu.

Making note of their orders, the waitress nodded and hurried away again.

"Well?" Ethan prodded.

She spoke brightly. "I was just wondering what our agenda is for today. Do you have an idea of where we should start?"

He frowned, making it clear he knew she was holding back, but he let it pass. "I thought we'd examine the accident site first, maybe get a feel for the surrounding area."

She nodded. "That sounds like a good place to start."

She suspected that it wouldn't be easy for Ethan to go to that spot. It might be less difficult for him if he could truly believe, as she did, that Kyle hadn't died there—but maybe not. Either way, Ethan had lost his little brother that day. Even if they did find him again, those missing years could never be recovered.

Their food was delivered with impressive

promptness, and they ate without much conversation. Aislinn's meal was very good, well cooked, nicely seasoned. The juicy chicken breast was accompanied by side orders of rice and steamed broccoli. Judging from the speed with which it disappeared, Ethan's lunch must have been good, too. The daily special turned out to be fried pork chops with red potatoes mashed with the skins, green beans and corn. Country cooking, just as the signs outside had advertised.

"You chose well," she said when they'd both eaten all they could. "That was delicious."

He shrugged. "You know what they say—if you want a decent meal, look for the place with the most pickup trucks in the parking lot."

She chuckled. "An interesting measure for culinary excellence."

A fleeting smile quirked his lips. "Probably not the best way to choose gourmet cuisine."

"True. But I'm not all that into gourmet cuisine, anyway. Though I do enjoy a place that serves interesting desserts," she added lightly.

"Even though you don't want to be a pastry chef in one of those snooty places."

She shrugged. "Doesn't mean I can't appreciate the efforts of the ones who do enjoy it."

"Can I get y'all some dessert?" their waitress asked, approaching the table again. "The coconut pie's good today. Got some chocolate cake, too."

Neither of them wanted dessert. "I'll take the check now," Ethan said.

Aislinn reached for her purse. "I'm paying my own way."

"I've got this." Obviously Ethan wasn't in the mood to argue about it just then.

Because she didn't want to cause a scene, Aislinn gave in, promising herself they would talk about the expenses of this trip later. While they were on a quest to find the truth about his brother, she had made the decision to accompany him. He hadn't offered to pay her, and she didn't want him to. Taking pay—even letting him buy her meals—felt too much like some of the "psychic" cons he'd been so leery of when he had first met her.

Aislinn was dressed in brown again. Ethan was beginning to seriously question her predilection for the rather drab color. Not that she could ever look drab, with that striking black hair and those dark chocolate eyes—but still. Remembering how good she had looked in the bold red of her bridesmaid dress, he wondered why she didn't choose bright colors more often.

"What's your favorite color?" he asked as he drove the windy mountain roads, breaking a silence between them that had stretched almost since they'd left the restaurant a half hour earlier.

The question seemed to startle her. He rather liked being able to take her by surprise occasionally.

"My favorite color? Why?"

"Just making small talk. You have a favorite color, don't you?"

"I—um…green. Emerald-green, a little brighter than your shirt."

"Really?" Seemed she could startle him a bit, too.

"Why does that surprise you?"

"I guess because I haven't seen any evidence of it. I've never seen you wear that color, didn't see it in your decorating, either, at your home or your shop."

She gave a self-conscious smile. "I don't have to wear it or decorate with it for it to be my favorite color. It just gives me pleasure to see it."

"Bet it would look good on you."

"It looks good on you. Green, I mean. What's *your* favorite color?" she asked quickly, as if to cover a slip of the tongue.

He didn't even have to stop to think about it. "It's red." As of fairly recently, actually.

"Do you wear red very often?"

Chuckling at the way she had turned the

question back against him, he admitted, "Not since I quit going to football games back home. The Danston Cardinals," he explained. "Everyone wears red."

"Actually, I knew that. Nic told me. It's why she picked red for her wedding color—because she and Joel fell in love during his homecoming weekend."

"Yeah, that was quite an event. Heidi, the class officer who arranges all those events, kept them busy partying all weekend—until the balcony collapse that last morning, anyway. That put an end to the reunion. It was a miracle no one was more badly injured."

Nodding her agreement, Aislinn asked, "Does your class have reunions?"

"Yeah."

"And do you go?"

He gave her a look that effectively answered her question.

"Oh," she said, smiling wryly. "Of course you don't."

"No. I see the people I want to see when I want to see them. As for sitting around with a group of near strangers, reminiscing about stuff we did twenty years ago, well, that would bore me into a coma."

"Somehow that doesn't surprise me."

"Has your class had a reunion yet?" He wasn't sure exactly how old she was, but he assumed she had to be close to Nic's age.

"They had a ten-year reunion last summer."

"I suppose you went?"

"No, actually. I skipped out on it."

Something in her voice made him glance her way. She was looking out the side window, so that all he could see of her face was her profile. Yet that was enough to let him see that she didn't really want to talk about her school years.

"Neither one of us is interested in reliving the past, I guess," he remarked lightly.

"I suppose not."

"So why are we making this trip?"

That made her look at him. "This isn't about the past," she reminded him. "Not primarily, anyway. It's about the present—and the future."

"So what do you see in my future? Do you predict that I'll find my brother and we'll all live happily ever after?"

"You'll find your brother. But whether you live happily ever after is up to you."

Inexplicably amused by her slightly acerbic tone, he chuckled. "Maybe I like being grouchy and bitter."

"Trust me, you wouldn't be the first person I know to enjoy living that way."

It was obvious that she was referring to someone in particular. One of her parents, maybe? Both?

He realized that he knew absolutely nothing about her past except that she had grown up in Cabot and had been friends with Nic for most of her life. Lizzie had implied that Aislinn's child-hood had been a difficult one, but he didn't know what that meant. How hard it had actually been.

Because this didn't seem to be the time to ask, he changed the subject. "Look at those directions I've written in that pad in the console, will you? I'm not sure where I'm supposed to turn once I get to Bellamy, the town where we lived. I looked up the directions on the Internet last night."

"Have you been back since you moved away?" she asked, opening the notepad.

"No. We moved three years after Kyle…disappeared and we never went back. I was nine. As far as I know, my parents pretty much lost contact with all their friends there, and we had no relatives there to visit."

If she had noticed his slight stammer about Kyle's fate, she didn't comment. "They wanted to start a new life in Alabama—away from people who knew them before they lost Kyle."

"Yeah, I guess. And it worked. We all made friends and felt at home there. Joel barely remembers living in North Carolina at all."

"But you do."

He shrugged. "I was older. But I wasn't opposed to the move. Even that young, I knew somehow that it would be easier for Mom to live in a new house, away from all the reminders of Kyle."

He paused a moment and then something made him add, "I still remember the day we moved into our house in Danston. Mom told us to choose our rooms. Joel looked up at her and asked which room was going to be Kyle's. I can still see her face when she told him that Kyle wouldn't have a room in the new house but he would always have a place in our hearts."

And then, embarrassed that he had revealed so much and wondering what it was about Aislinn that brought out things like that from him, he spoke again before she could comment. "So where do I turn? It's a highway number, I think."

Probably sensing that he needed the change of topic, she began to read the directions to him.

* * *

Ethan guided the rented vehicle to the curb and put it into Park. "That's it. That's the house where we lived."

Aislinn studied the tidy redbrick, ranch-style house across the street. The trim and shutters were cream, as were the posts that supported the roof of the long front porch. A redwood fence surrounded the backyard, but the neatly manicured front lawn was open and inviting, with a couple of large shade trees and flowers in well-tended beds.

Whoever owned the place now took pride in their home and kept it looking nice. It appeared much the same way when the Brannons had lived here, Aislinn thought. There had been toys on the lawn and a swing set in the backyard. A happy home but a noisy one, with three boisterous little boys inside.

It had been very quiet in that house after Kyle's disappearance, she thought sadly. While the laughter had gradually returned, the tone had forever been altered. The family's broken hearts had mended but had never been made completely whole again. And no matter what happened in the future, those scars would never completely heal.

"Your Christmas tree was always in that window," she said, pointing. "And you had a dog. A small brown one."

"A dachshund," he confirmed. "We called him Teddy."

She could almost see him, a dark-haired little boy chasing after a small, brown dog. "You had a hiding place in the backyard."

"There was a big bush. The branches came all the way down to the ground, and I could hide inside them and watch people without them seeing me." He looked at her as he spoke, evidently trying to determine if she was only guessing or if it was more than that.

"You went there a lot after Kyle left. And you took something of his in there with you."

"A toy," he said, speaking more slowly now.

"A stuffed cat. I thought if I concentrated really hard on the toy, Kyle would come home. He'd be okay, and my parents would stop crying."

"You kept that cat. Even when your parents packed away Kyle's things, you kept the toy and you didn't tell them. You took it with you when you moved—because you thought as long as you kept it, there was always a chance Kyle would come home to claim it. Do you still have it?"

"No."

She frowned. "Yes, you do. It's packed away. You haven't looked at it in a long time. But you have it."

"Okay, I do," he admitted a bit crossly. "How do you know these things, Aislinn?"

She was appalled to feel her eyes suddenly fill with hot tears. "I don't know," she whispered.

Visibly rattled, he asked quickly, "You aren't going to cry, are you?"

Forcing her eyes to dry, she shook her head. "No. Sorry."

She didn't know how to explain her uncharacteristic emotionalism. Part of it was because of the vague images that had filled her mind. The sad little boy grieving for his lost brother. The happy family whose lives had been so tragically and so permanently changed.

She was also genuinely unnerved by the clarity of the images she was receiving. She didn't see the need to tell him again that she didn't usually pick up so much information. That the past few weeks had been different for her—and more than a little frightening.

She had learned to live with what she considered heightened intuition. She had never asked for more. Never wanted more.

Clearing her throat, she spoke more brusquely. "So Carmen left here with your brother that afternoon. In the rain, knowing there was extensive flooding in the area."

Seeming relieved by the return to objective facts, Ethan nodded. "Yeah. She left the house at about two o'clock that afternoon. One of the neighbors saw her drive away and thought it was strange that she would go out in that weather."

"When did the anonymous call come in about the car going off the road?"

"An hour and a half later. Just after three-thirty."

"It took her that long to get there?"

"We'll find out. We're going to drive there from here."

"Were any of her things missing? Clothing, money, that sort of thing?"

"I don't know yet. If so, Mom didn't seem to know anything about it."

"From what we saw in the newspaper accounts, there didn't seem to be much of an investigation. It appeared to be taken as fact that the car went over and the bodies were washed away."

"There was no real reason to think otherwise. Carmen had been our nanny for eighteen months. She seemed perfectly content with her life. She had no money, nowhere to go. Why would she have faked her death?"

"Maybe you'll have the chance to ask her." But something about that statement didn't feel right. Maybe he would never find her. Or maybe Carmen had died since. Except for the picture of Kyle she had drawn in her sleep, she had no insight into what had become of Carmen or Kyle since they'd disappeared into that storm.

Ethan put the car into gear. "Let's find the spot where the car went over. Check your watch. We'll see how long it takes to get there from here."

"It was somewhere along this stretch of road. I'm not sure exactly where."

A metal guardrail provided a border between the two-lane highway and the steep drop-off to the river below. Ethan had already informed her that the river was popular for canoeing and kayaking in the shallows and white-water areas and for fishing in the deeper parts. It was deeper in this area, the ever-moving surface glittering in the late-afternoon sun, a few fishing boats tucked into small inlets or drifting with the current. She pictured it as it had been on that afternoon, swollen several feet above its current level, rushing violently downstream and carrying anything in its path along with it.

Glancing at her watch, she said, "We've driven twenty-five minutes from the house. There's no way it took her almost an hour and a half to get here."

Doing his own mental calculations, he nodded. "Even in the bad weather, it shouldn't have taken her that long. Either she drove a more circuitous path to get here, for some reason, or she made a stop along the way."

He pulled over to the narrow shoulder and stopped the car. "This guardrail wasn't here thirty years ago. Just the shoulder and then the drop-off. The newspaper report said there weren't any skid marks from braking—though the water on the road could have had something to do with that, if she hydroplaned."

Gazing at the river, Aislinn chewed her lower lip, trying to visualize the accident.

"Well?" he prompted after a moment. "Are you picking up anything?"

She turned to look at him. "'Picking up anything?'"

"You know. Getting any additional information by being here at the actual site. Like you did at the house."

She supposed she couldn't blame him for asking. She had sensed several details at the house that he hadn't told her. Turning toward the river again, she tried to focus. Open her mind.

"Well?" he asked again.

Sighing, she shook her head. "I don't know what I'm supposed to be doing. I just feel kind of foolish, like I'm—I don't know—playing psychic or something."

"What were you doing when that stuff came to you back at the house?"

"Nothing. I just looked at the house and I

saw the Christmas tree and the puppy. And you, hiding in the backyard."

He looked beyond her to the river, then put the car into gear again. "Let's try something. Keep looking out the window."

"What?"

"Just let me know if you get anything," he said, pulling back onto the highway and proceeding slowly down the road.

She wasn't sure what he was talking about, but she cooperated by gazing out the passenger window, watching the river go by. The passing scenery was rather mesmerizing, and she could feel her thoughts drifting like the lazy current.

Until she suddenly went tense and said, "Here. Pull over."

They were perhaps a mile and a half farther than before. Glancing into the rearview mirror to make sure no one was coming up behind them, Ethan drove onto the shoulder again and pushed the gearshift into Park.

The road was a bit wider here, with shoulder on both sides and a clear view of the river. No trees to impede the view, or to have stopped a car had there not been a guardrail.

"It happened here," she said, staring at the water with a heavy feeling in her chest.

"What exactly happened?" He spoke very quietly, matter-of-factly, neither belief nor skepticism audible in his tone.

She frowned. "There was another car."

"Someone ran her off the road?"

"No."

"The witness was driving the other car? The woman who called in the accident?"

"I don't—no."

"Then what is it about the other car?"

Dragging her gaze from the river with an effort, she looked at him instead. He was watching her closely, his expression unreadable but his body tense behind the steering wheel.

She wished she could know what he was thinking. But because he seemed to be willing to listen to what she said, she told him what she had just realized. "Someone picked her up here. Her and Kyle."

"After the accident, you mean?"

She shook her head. "They never went into the river, Ethan. There was no accident. The car was deliberately pushed over the side, and she and Kyle left the scene in someone else's car. I think Carmen was the anonymous woman who called the police."

Chapter Eleven

"Cassandra. Cassandra, can you hear me?"

She opened her eyes blearily, wondering why the voice sounded so strange and hollow. Why it was so hard to clear her vision. To clear her mind.

"There you are. Can you see my face? Do you know who I am?"

Blinking a couple of times, she forced herself to focus. "Dr. Thomas. What are you—what's going on?"

He patted her hand, and she realized that his smile was strained, his face tight. "The staff couldn't wake you," he explained quietly. "You were out so deeply that they were getting ready to call for an ambulance by the time I arrived."

"No. No ambulance. I don't want to go to a hospital. I'm fine."

Slipping his stethoscope into his ears, he pressed the bell to her chest. "I'll be the judge of that."

She concentrated on keeping her breathing and heart rate steady. Calm. "I'm fine," she repeated evenly. "I guess I was just really tired. I haven't been sleeping well lately, you know."

"Cassandra, that was more than just sleeping. You were unconscious. But your heart sounds good," he conceded slowly, wrapping the stethoscope around his neck again. "Your blood pressure is normal."

"Perhaps it was a reaction to the new medication," she suggested.

"Maybe." But he didn't look convinced, and she was beginning to worry that he was still considering hospitalization.

"I really do feel fine," she said. "Why don't we give it a few hours and let me prove that there's no lasting effect? It isn't as if I won't have people to check in on me."

He nodded reluctantly. "If that's what you want."

"It's what I want. Please."

Sighing, he gave in. "All right. We'll see how it goes."

Relief flooded through her. "May I have a glass of water? I'm really quite thirsty."

"Of course." Glancing around at the nurse who'd hovered behind him, the doctor satisfied himself that water was being fetched before turning back to Cassandra. He sat on the side of the bed, the concern slowly fading from his face. "You gave us quite a scare."

She smiled briefly. "I'm sorry. It wasn't intentional."

"You've been feeling well lately? No shortness of breath? No dizziness?"

"Except for a few episodes of insomnia, I've been very well. No complaints at all."

Those too-perceptive eyes searched her face. "And when you do sleep, do you dream?"

An odd question. She mulled it over for a moment while she sipped the water the nurse had given her before leaving to take care of other duties. She wasn't sure how to respond. It wouldn't be with the truth. "Sometimes. Nothing particularly interesting. But no nightmares like before, if that's what you're asking."

A lie, of course. But if it kept her out of the hospital, she considered it justifiable.

Still in that casually conversational tone, he asked, "Do you dream of the past or the present?"

Not certain where he was going with this, she shrugged lightly against the pillows. "I don't remember, exactly. Just dreams."

"Many of the residents here dream of their childhood, you know. They tell me about reliving some of their happiest moments when they're asleep."

"Lucky them to have had such happy childhoods to relive."

"Does that mean your own wasn't so happy?"

She merely looked at him.

"Ah. Now you've gone quiet again."

"I can't say the same for you."

He chuckled. "Always have a comeback, don't you?"

"Oh, I try."

"I'd like to think we've become friends, you and I."

"I'm very fond of you, Dr. Thomas."

"Then why won't you talk to me? Tell me a little about yourself?"

"Why is it so important to you to hear about my past?"

"Because I think it's haunting you," he replied simply. "I think you've been carrying some very heavy baggage that's weighing you down now, causing you a great deal of pain. And it seems to be getting heavier, for some reason. I'd like to help you with that load if I can, Cassandra."

"You're a fine young man," she told him, touched by the sincerity in his voice. "You care very deeply about your patients. Too much, perhaps. But there comes a time when all of us must accept that we've done as much as we can. There's nothing you can do for me, Dr. Thomas, except to take care of my physical health, as you do the other residents here."

"I'm not sure I can accept that."

She shrugged again.

He shifted and reached for the chart that had rested beside him on the bed. "The medical history you've given us is far from complete, but from what I've read, you've had a difficult time of it even before you were stricken with MS."

"I've had my share of ailments." Some of which she had brought on herself, through dangerous and self-destructive behavior. That was before she had learned to accept—and forgive—herself.

"You told me you married your last

husband when you were fifty. Were you ever married before?"

"Once. Briefly. What about you, Dr. Thomas? Ever come close to getting married yourself?"

She could see that he was on the verge of telling her that they were talking about her, not him—but then he seemed to think better of it. Perhaps it occurred to him that she would be more likely to share if he did. "I almost asked someone to marry me once."

"Really? Why didn't you?"

He chuckled. "Someone else beat me to it."

"Then you weren't meant to be with her."

"That's what I told myself at the time. Didn't stop me from kicking myself for waiting too late, though."

"You'll find someone else." She had no doubt of that.

"Maybe. I'm not in any hurry, though I wouldn't mind having a family someday." Turning that into a smooth segue, he asked, "You never had children with your first husband?"

She turned her head on the pillow, looking away from him, trying to hide the sharp pain that went through her in response to his question. It wasn't the type of pain that he could treat, so there was no need to burden him with it. "I'd like to get up now, Dr. Thomas. Would you mind sending someone in to help me on your way out?"

He sat without moving for a few moments longer, obviously aware that he had just been gently dismissed. And then he stood, looking grave. "I'll be back to check on you this evening. And I'll probably have you monitored periodically during the night, just to make sure you don't slip too deeply into unconsciousness again. In the meantime, if you need anything, anything at all, have someone contact me, will you?"

"Thank you, Dr. Thomas. I want you to know that I deeply appreciate your concern. There haven't been many people who have cared for me as sweetly as you have."

He leaned over to touch her cheek, the gesture so tender that it almost brought tears to her jaded eyes. "Someday you'll feel like talking to me, Cassandra. And then maybe we'll find a way to take some of that weight off your shoulders. You must be awfully tired of carrying it by now."

"Go take care of Mrs. Kennedy," she said, her voice a bit hoarse as she blurted the first thing that came to her mind in an attempt to control her strained emotions. "She's not doing so well today. She needs you worse than I do."

He straightened. "Now how would you know that? You've only just started the day."

"I, um—she was feeling poorly yesterday. I don't expect she's any better today."

"I'll go check on her. Remember, call if you need me."

"I will. Thank you."

She watched the door close behind him and only then did she allow herself to swipe at her eyes. She would never reveal all the details of her past, of course. Dr. Thomas would never understand—and she couldn't bear to see the disillusionment in those gentle eyes if he ever learned the truth.

It was hard enough for her to remember the things she had done before she had taken the name Cassandra and created yet another new life for herself.

"Where do you want me to put your bags?"

Aislinn looked rather blankly around the nondescript motel room, then waved a hand toward one of the two beds. "Just put them there."

It was one of the handful of complete sentences she had uttered in the past hour, since they'd left the spot by the river and had driven back into town. She'd had no comment about the motel he had selected, speaking up only to insist on paying for her own room. And now she stood in the center of her room, frowning at her bags as if she had never seen them before.

She was pale again, he noted, studying her face. The skin around her mouth was tight, as if she were holding her emotions in check by force. He thought again that she would have to be an extremely gifted actress to be faking her reactions to the visions she'd been having—or whatever he should call them.

He was a long way from believing that what she had told him was anything more than figments of an overactive imagination, but he conceded that she seemed to believe everything she said. Whatever she was going through while she struggled with these episodes, it looked real. And obviously difficult for her.

"Do you want to rest a while before dinner? We can start tomorrow looking for people who knew Carmen."

"I, um—whatever you want to do."

"Get some rest. I'll be next door if you need me."

She nodded but remained where she stood.

He moved toward the door, then paused before opening it. He felt funny leaving her here like this, so dazed and wan. "Aislinn."

"Yes?"

"Are you okay?"

"Yes, I'm fine," she said in that same monotone.

He sighed and moved back toward her. Taking her arm, he guided her to the bed and put both hands on her shoulders, pushing downward until she sat on the edge. "Lie down."

She blinked a couple of times, rousing a bit. "What?"

"Lie down," he repeated, punctuating the command with another little shove that tumbled her backward against the pillow. Lifting her feet, he removed her shoes, tossed them on the floor and then stepped backward. "Get some rest."

She started to say something and then she fell silent, curling one hand beneath her cheek as she turned on her side and closed her eyes. He thought she might be asleep by the time he reached the door.

He stood there for a few more moments, just looking at her. She was absolutely one of the most beautiful women he'd ever met. He wouldn't have been a normal, straight male had the thought of joining her there in that cozy bed not crossed his mind. But talk about complications...

Pushing a hand through his hair, he let himself out of the room, closing the door silently behind him.

Aislinn woke with a start, not quite certain where she was. She was wearing her clothes, though her feet were bare, and she lay on top of the covers. There was a light shining in her eyes.

Pushing her hair out of her face, she sat up, only to find herself facing the chair in which Ethan sat reading a newspaper. His long legs were stretched out in front of him, feet crossed at the ankles, and he looked quite comfortable there in her room. *Why* was he there in her room?

He looked up in response to her movement. Checking her face with a shrewd glance, he nodded in satisfaction. "You look better."

She had only a vague memory of checking in. Of being urged by Ethan to take a nap. It embarrassed her now to think about how out of it she had been.

"What are you doing in here?"

Setting the newspaper aside, he straightened in the chair. "You were sleeping so heavily I was a little concerned about you. You've been out for several hours."

It was unlike her to sleep so deeply that he had been able to enter her room without rousing her. It made her uncomfortable to think that he'd been there watching her sleep, even though she was touched that he'd done so out of concern.

"I don't know why I was so tired," she said, swinging her feet to the floor. "I hardly ever do that."

"Are you hungry?"

She pressed a hand to her stomach. "Actually, yes, I am. What time is it?"

"It's almost eight o'clock." He turned to the small, round table tucked into the corner and picked up a white paper bag. "I didn't know if you would want to go back out tonight, so I brought food."

"That sounds good. Give me a minute to freshen up."

He nodded. "I'll go get some cold drinks out of the vending machine. What do you want?"

"Anything diet."

"I'll be right back."

As she washed her hands a few minutes later, it occurred to her to wonder how he had gotten into her room while she was sleeping. The door automatically locked when closed. The only explanation was that he had taken her key with him.

At least he knocked when he came back from fetching drinks. Crossing the room to let him in, she had the uncomfortable suspicion that he had knocked, before, too, but that she'd been sleeping too deeply to hear him. No wonder he'd been concerned about her.

They sat on opposite sides of the little table, knees almost touching as Ethan pulled food out of the bag. As he unwrapped deli sandwiches, he explained that he'd chosen something that didn't have to be served warm. Turkey, cheese, lettuce and tomato on whole-wheat bread, along with two bags of baked potato chips. For dessert, he'd purchased two white-chocolate-and-macadamia-nut cookies.

Aislinn picked up her sandwich. "This looks very good."

"I figured you wouldn't mind a light dinner since we had a heavier lunch."

"I don't mind at all." It was funny how ravenous she was all of a sudden. She ate the sandwich and all the chips, then started on the cookie, washing it all down with the diet soda Ethan had brought her.

She looked up to find him watching her. Self-conscious now, she wiped cookie crumbs from her fingers. "I was hungry."

"I noticed."

"It was good," she said, reaching for her soda can. "Thank you."

"You're welcome. So what happened to you this afternoon, Aislinn?"

She had been expecting the question. She wished she knew how to answer it. "I'm not sure, exactly."

"You keep saying this is all different for you. Does that include the way you zoned out after having those visions by the river?"

"They weren't—" She had started to speak automatically, but she stopped herself, knowing that this time she wouldn't have been telling the truth. They *had* been visions. There was no other way to refer to them. "No. Nothing like that has happened to me before."

"You really believe the things you saw are true?"

"You can confirm part of them," she

reminded him. "Everything I saw at the house. As for what I learned at the river, yes, I believe it's true. Carmen Nichols faked her own death and kidnapped your brother. Someone helped her. I don't know who. I don't know where they went when they left there. But I know that's the way it happened."

"And you expect me to believe it, too. Just because you say so."

She sighed, thinking that they had been over this too many times already. "Believe what you want, Ethan. I'm only trying to help."

He leaned back in his chair, slinging one arm over the back, his expression thoughtful. "Has it occurred to you that you continually send me mixed signals? Even as you continue to deny that you are a psychic or a seer or whatever people might call it, you tell me you somehow know things you couldn't possibly know without some sort of extrasensory perception. You tell me you're simply a good guesser, but then you ask me to accept that you are absolutely certain that Carmen stole my brother."

Nervously gathering the debris from their casual meal, she nodded. "I can't blame you for being confused. I'm pretty bewildered myself by all of this."

He thought about that, then asked, "Why do you fight it so hard? Your ability, I mean."

She flinched. "Wouldn't you? Would you want to be seen as a freak? An oddity?"

"I've been considered an oddity for most of my life," he answered with a shrug. "People don't understand why I'm not interested in amassing a fortune for myself. Why I choose to live quietly, in solitude for the most part. Why I don't play the social games most people choose to play."

"But you came from a good family. You live the way you do out of choice, not because there's something 'strange' about you. People may call you odd or antisocial, but they don't call you 'spooky.'"

A muscle twitched in his jaw, letting her know that the label rang a bell with him. Either he'd already heard someone refer to her that way or he had thought it himself. Maybe both.

"You haven't said much about your family," he commented instead.

She hadn't said anything about her family, actually. And she wasn't sure she wanted to do so now.

And yet…she was aware that she and Ethan had been discussing the most intimate details of his own family's past, things that had to have been painful for him to share with her. She doubted that anyone else knew he still had Kyle's stuffed cat tucked away in his possessions, yet she had forced that admission out of him by confronting him with what she had seen. Despite his expressed doubts, he was here, looking into the things she had told him, on the off chance that she could actually be right.

The least she could do would be to tell him

a little more about herself, since she was asking him to have so much faith in her word, she thought reluctantly.

"I don't talk about my family much because it's too painful," she confessed.

"Then forget I mentioned it," he said immediately. "We'll talk about something else."

She suspected that he wanted to change the subject as much for his benefit as for her own. Ethan wasn't comfortable with delving into emotions, as witnessed by his near panic when he'd seen the threat of tears in her eyes. That was probably a result of surviving too many emotional scenes in his past, when his family had lost their youngest child and, later, Joel's beloved first wife.

"It's okay," she assured him with a slight smile. "I don't mind so much telling you about it."

Still looking a bit doubtful, he nodded.

Aislinn drew a deep breath. "I should start with my grandmother, I suppose. She died before I was born," she said, keeping her tone even, impassive. "Everyone said she was a troubled woman who suffered from bouts of depression. She died of a heart attack just after her fortieth birthday."

"That must have been hard on her family."

She nodded. "My grandmother was an only child whose own parents both died relatively young. She and Granddad married when she was in her early twenties. From the few stories I heard about their marriage, it wasn't a particularly happy one. Granddad was a rather humorless man, hardworking, extremely religious, old-fashioned when it came to gender roles. He didn't know what to do with my grandmother during her 'spells,' so he pretty much let her suffer through them on her own."

"How many children did they have?"

"Just the one. My mother."

"Having a child didn't make your grandmother happier?"

"I'm afraid not. And my mother wasn't an

easy child. She was unruly, stubborn, rebelli-ous. Maybe it was her nature, maybe a result of the way they raised her—or a combination of all those things—but by the time she was twelve she was already sneaking out at night, running wild with kids who were a lot older than she was, regularly getting into trouble with the law. I was told that my grandfather tried everything he could think of to straighten her out, from preaching to punishment to coun-seling, which wasn't exactly common in the early sixties—but nothing worked."

Ethan took a sip of his soda without com-menting, though Aislinn knew he was absorb-ing every word.

"My mother was fifteen when her mother died. A lot of people blamed it on her—includ-ing my grandfather, I think. Maybe he never told her so, but she probably suspected it."

Wincing, Ethan muttered, "Rough on her."

"Yes. It must have been horrible for her. Anyway, after that, she went completely out of control. My grandfather washed his hands of her a year later."

"She was on her own at sixteen?"

She nodded.

"And then she had you."

He was obviously envisioning a teenage pregnancy. Logical assumption, but she shook her head. "Not for another sixteen years."

That made his eyebrows shoot up in surprise. "She was thirty-two when you were born?"

"Yes. She would be sixty now. About the same age as the nanny who took Kyle, I guess."

"What happened during those years before you were born?"

"She took off right after Granddad threw her out, and no one heard from her in all those years. And then she showed up with me. Granddad was seventy, still living in the same house where he'd raised my mother. He still owned and operated the hardware store he'd bought just before my mother was born. Granddad was stunned to see his daughter after all those years, but he welcomed her home and invited her to stay with him as long as she needed to. He once told me that he loved me from the moment he saw me. He said I looked like his mother, whereas my mother looked like his late wife."

"What was your mother's name?" he asked, as if suddenly realizing that she hadn't mentioned it before.

"She was christened Mary Alice Flaherty. When she was six, she insisted on answering to Maxie. At fourteen, she became Butterfly. Remember, this was during the early hippie years, a culture she embraced wholeheartedly."

"Butterfly Flaherty." He shook his head. "And people called her that?"

"Her friends did, I guess. Her father called her Mary Alice."

"So then she came back to town, carrying you," he prompted, totally into the story now.

"Right. She used the nickname Allie then. She was past thirty but still eccentric. The way she was described to me, her hair was waist-length and dyed bright red. She wore peasant clothes and sandals and she was driving a '69 VW van. I was six months old."

"Your father?"

"She never mentioned him," she said with the slight pang that always accompanied the awareness that she would never know her father. "She told my grandfather that it wasn't relevant. He rarely talked about my mother to me, but I once heard him mention to my aunt that my mother had implied there had been another child—a boy—that she had abandoned. That she still felt guilty about leaving behind. He told my aunt that he couldn't believe then that his daughter would have abandoned a child, but when she did basically the same with me, he figured it was probably true."

She cleared her throat, trying not to think about lonely childhood longings. "Granddad never knew I heard him say that, but I was pretty stunned by the revelation. It's possible I have a brother somewhere I've never met. I don't know for certain, but then, I've never been able to sense much of importance about anything that matters most to me."

"But your mother chose to keep you."

"She said she'd wanted to try to be a mother to me but she'd realized she couldn't handle it alone."

"So she stayed in town then? Raised you with her father's assistance?"

"No." She laced her fingers together on the tabletop, trying to keep the pain in her heart out of her voice. "Apparently they spent a very strained evening together, and then she left town again before dawn the next morning. Alone."

Chapter Twelve

She had caught him by surprise again. "She left you with your grandfather?"

"She didn't even tell him she was leaving," she added grimly. "He woke up the next morning to find her van gone and me crying in the playpen she'd put me to sleep in. She didn't even leave a note, but Granddad said he knew when he saw me that she wouldn't be back."

"What kind of mother would do something like that?"

"Mine."

The stark reply hung in the air for a moment before he asked, "So you were raised by your grandfather?"

"Believe it or not, yes. He had a younger sister, Maureen, who'd been widowed a few years earlier. She moved in with him to help raise me. She was in her early sixties, and her own son was long grown."

"Still, they were both fairly old to become responsible for a six-month-old baby."

"There were people who suggested that they should give me up for adoption, but they both refused. I think my grandfather felt guilty that he'd failed with my mother. As for Aunt Maureen, she was lonely and at loose ends since losing her husband and she told me later that I gave her new purpose in her life. Her son, my cousin Alex, was and still is a confirmed bachelor, so she didn't expect grandchildren. She and Granddad both saw me as a way to atone for past parenting mistakes, I guess."

"A big load for a small girl to carry."

She shrugged.

His eyes grave, he asked, "What was your childhood like?"

"Quiet. Orderly. I had everything I needed."

"Not everything."

Because she couldn't really argue with that, she let his comment slide. "I was a very good child," she informed him. "I never broke the rules, never talked back, never missed curfew."

"That doesn't surprise me," he murmured.

She drew another deep breath. Since she had told him so much already, she might as well tell him the rest. "When I was five, I told my grandfather that the house across the street was going to burn down. Two days later, it did."

"How did he react to that?"

"With fear. And anger. He ordered me to close my mind to thoughts like that. He said they were unnatural. Probably unholy. And that they could only lead me into misery and isolation."

Ethan rubbed his chin thoughtfully. "Your grandmother had the gift?"

"Probably."

"Your mother?"

She nodded. "Whenever I slipped during my childhood and said something I shouldn't have known, Granddad gave me the lecture again. He said my mother had always pretended to be 'special' and that it had only led her into trouble. He said he had tried to punish those thoughts out of her and it hadn't worked, so with me he wanted to use reason. Logic. He told me no one would like me if they thought I was weird. That people would be afraid of me. Or that they would try to use me to their own advantage. He told me that I should pray every night to be normal."

Ethan said something beneath his breath that might have been a curse.

"He meant well," she said wearily. "He'd seen his wife descend into depression and his daughter lose herself in drugs and rebellion. He didn't want the same things to happen to me."

"So you listened to him."

"Yes. I worked even harder to be the perfect child. But I wasn't very good at being 'normal,'" she added with just a touch of bitterness. "I didn't always know I was saying something that other people would find strange. So I quit talking much at all, which made me even more of an oddball among my age group. Nic was the first person I met who never seemed to find me strange. Who accepted my occasional insights with such matter-of-factness that it made me feel almost average."

"You continued to live with your great-aunt after your grandfather died?"

"Yes. She was in good health until I turned seventeen, when she suffered a mild stroke. I took care of her during my senior year of high school and for six months after my graduation. She suffered another stroke then. A fatal one."

"That's why you didn't go to college. You were taking care of your aunt."

"She took care of me all those years. It seemed only right."

Ethan was quiet for so long that Aislinn became self-conscious again. What was he thinking? She didn't want his pity; that wasn't the reason she'd told him the things she had. She certainly didn't want him to wonder about things like hereditary mental illnesses. He wouldn't be the first to mention that possibility.

After another few moments he said, "You've had an interesting life."

She was surprised into a weak smile. "Not so much. I told you, I've lived very quietly. I discovered my talent for cake decorating when I was in my teens and I parlayed it into a career. I learned to interact better with people through my business and I've made a few good friends. I'm quite content, but my life is hardly noteworthy. I suppose my mother was the one whose life could be considered interesting."

"Is she still living?"

"I don't know."

"You've never heard from her?"

"I got a birthday card from her on my tenth

birthday. All it said was, 'I think about you every day.' Granddad and Aunt Maureen considered not giving it to me because they thought it might upset me, but eventually they decided to show it to me and warn me not to read too much into it."

"It must have meant something to you for her to tell you she hadn't forgotten you."

"I wasn't sure how I felt about it," she admitted. "In some ways, it was harder to know that she hadn't forgotten me but she still chose not to see me. I still wonder what became of her. Why she left me with her father, whom she never got along with herself."

"If it's true that she knew things, maybe she somehow understood that you would be better off there. That you would grow up safe and relatively happy there. You can't argue that you've turned out well. You have friends, a nice home, a successful business. You probably had a much better life than you'd have had with her, drifting around in an old VW van."

"You're right, of course." But there had been many times in her quiet, predictable, ordinary life when she had fantasized about being on the road with her wild, free-spirited, adventurous mother.

"Did she name you?"

"Yes. I was lucky, I guess, that she didn't name me Rainbow or Strawberry or Moonbeam, not that Granddad would have left it at that. Aislinn isn't exactly a common name in Arkansas, but at least it sounds like a name. Even my middle name is ordinary enough."

"Joy," he said, proving that he remembered. "Much better than *my* middle name."

Intrigued, she cocked her head. "What is yours?"

His mouth twisted. "Albert."

She didn't laugh. But it took an effort. "You don't really look like an Albert."

"It was my grandfather's name. My paternal grandfather. He lived in Michigan with his third wife. We used to go visit him when I was a kid. He had a fishing cabin on a lake that I thought was the greatest place in the world. I always said that when I grew up I was going to live in a house just like it."

"And do you?"

"Pretty close. I've got a house on a river. You can fish off the dock in my backyard. Sit outside in the evenings and watch deer walk along the riverbanks."

"It must be lovely."

"I like it."

She stood to throw away the trash from their dinner. "Well, now you know my entire life story," she said lightly. "Sorry you asked?"

He didn't smile. "No."

"Anything else you want to know?"

"How can you know what happened to Kyle and not know whether your own mother is still living? Or whether she had any other children?"

She sank onto the foot of the bed, resting her hands on either side of her. "As I said, I almost never get any feelings that affect myself. I don't know why I pick up some things and not others. It seems to be completely random and usually pretty vague. Today was literally the first time in my life I've been able to deliberately focus and pick up such clear details."

"Doing so seemed to take a lot out of you. You went out like a light when we got here."

"I felt completely drained," she admitted. "It was a little unnerving, actually."

"Tell me about it."

She cleared her throat. "Sorry if I worried you."

He inclined his head. "I don't know what to make of you," he said after another pause. "I still have trouble believing that you can somehow know all these things."

"That's understandable. I just hope you no longer think I'm some sort of con artist. Or crazy."

"I don't think you're a con artist."

After another moment she smiled ruefully. "I

notice you didn't reassure me about the craziness part."

He pushed his chair back from the table and stood, looking down at her with an expression she couldn't quite decipher. "I told you once that I thought maybe we're both crazy. The more we get into this bizarre investigation, the more I wonder if I was right."

Rising, she gazed up at him. "You came here because, even though it's hard for you to believe, you had to know if there was a chance I'm right about Kyle."

"Yeah. I guess."

"What other reason would there be?"

He reached out to cup her cheek in one hand. "You can't think of any other reason I'd want to spend time with you?"

Warmth flooded through her, centering in the skin beneath his palm. She blurted the first words that came into her mind. "You think I'm spooky."

"Hell, yeah."

Her sputtered laugh was smothered beneath his mouth when he lowered his head to hers.

Aislinn's slender body arrowed neatly into the water of the swimming pool, creating hardly a splash. Standing in the shadows of the motel building, Ethan watched her begin to swim laps, her strokes steady and strong. She seemed to be working off some sort of tension.

He knew the feeling.

She was the only one in the pool. Technically it was after hours, and the pool was closed, though no effort was made by management to stop late swimmers. She shouldn't be out alone at night like this. He supposed she felt relatively safe because of the motel rooms surrounding the pool, but it still wasn't a good idea. Crossing his arms over his chest, he leaned against the wall, silently standing guard.

Watching over her was hardly a hardship. He didn't think he'd ever seen anything more beautiful than Aislinn moving so sleekly through the glistening, softly lit pool water. She was modestly dressed in a one-piece black bathing suit—another example of her habit of dressing to fade into the background. He could have told her she was wasting her time. Aislinn could wear a sheet of burlap and still catch the eyes of every man within sight of her.

He understood now why she worked so hard to blend into the crowd. She had been abandoned by her mother and raised by aging relatives who'd done their best to drill the uniqueness out of her. *Different* was a pejorative to her. *Average* a compliment.

She did a practiced turn at the deep end of the pool and swam in the other direction. He'd heard her leave her room earlier, an hour after he'd surprised them both with a good-night kiss. He had been tempted to follow that kiss up with more…and then some…but a remaining shred of common sense had given him the strength to pull away, to tell her good-night and walk out of the room. She hadn't tried to detain him.

This wasn't a woman he wanted to get involved with. For one thing, Aislinn wasn't the no-strings-dalliance sort. She came with complications he had assiduously avoided during the past few years. Not to mention the complications that had to do with Aislinn herself.

He was giving her a few more days to show him any evidence that Kyle was still alive, and then he was putting both her and her psychic claims out of his mind, he promised himself. That was the best he could do—even if it was taking every ounce of self-control he possessed to keep himself from taking her slim, wet body into his arms and making them both forget about anything beyond tonight.

Wrapping herself in a large towel, Aislinn slid her feet into sandals and shook her dripping hair out of her face. The grounds of the little, out-of-the-way motel were quiet, pretty much deserted at this hour, but she wasn't concerned for her safety. Her room was only a few steps away.

She had needed the exercise of swimming. Maybe she'd slept too long that afternoon or maybe she was still keyed up from her talk with Ethan. Or from something else with Ethan. But after he'd left her, she'd been filled with pent-up energy that no amount of pacing the small confines of her room could burn off. Looking out her window, she'd seen the pool and had impulsively changed into the bathing suit she had packed at the last minute.

The swim had helped. A little. Maybe she would be able to sleep now. If she could find a way to prevent the memory of Ethan's kiss from keeping her awake all night.

Fat chance.

She moved toward her room, resigned to a restless night. Her breath caught when someone moved out of the nearby shadows.

"You really shouldn't be out here by yourself at night," Ethan said, his expression grim when the light fell on his face. "Especially since you're no good at seeing your own future."

Trying to steady her racing heart, she cleared her throat. "You startled me. But I was ready to run and scream if I had to."

"If I'd been someone who wanted to hurt you, I wouldn't have given you a chance to run or scream," he pointed out.

He stood between her and her door. She took a step toward him. "Then it's a good thing you don't want to hurt me, isn't it?"

"Yeah." His voice was rougher now. "I guess it is."

The same restless energy that had driven her into the pool impelled her forward. He remained where he stood until she stopped, inches away from him. The cool water still dripped from her hair and slid down her body. She could almost fancy that it evaporated in the heat of Ethan's gaze.

Sliding a hand up his arm and around to the back of his neck, she lifted herself onto tiptoes and pressed her wet body against his dry one. Her lips only a breath from his, she asked, "How are you at telling the future, Ethan?"

"Not worth a damn," he muttered hoarsely.

"So I guess you weren't expecting me to do this," she murmured and pressed her mouth to his.

"No," he said when she gave him a chance to speak a few moments later. "I wasn't expecting that."

"Then this should come as a real surprise to you." She wrapped both arms around his neck and kissed him again.

With a low laugh deep in his chest, he pulled her closer, smothering her mouth beneath his.

"I wasn't going to do this." Ethan's voice was low, his expression rueful as he loomed over her.

Lying on her back on her bed, she reached up to him. "Neither was I."

He slid the straps of her bathing suit off her

shoulders, lowering his lips to her still-damp skin. "Probably not a good idea."

Arching her neck to give him better access, she sighed. "No, probably not."

"There's still time to come to our senses."

She nuzzled her cheek against his soft brown hair. "You first."

He pushed her suit farther down and groaned. "Maybe it's too late after all."

Offering herself to him, she closed her eyes. "Definitely too late."

Drifting in a haze of satisfaction, Aislinn forced her eyelids open when the bed shifted. "Where are you going?"

Reaching for his clothes, Ethan replied, "I'm heading for my room. Get some sleep. We'll get an early start in the morning."

Lifting herself to one elbow, she pulled the sheet across her and watched him dress. "Second thoughts?"

"Second. Third. Fourth."

She couldn't be offended since she felt much the same way. "You don't have to worry about it, Ethan. I'm not going to cause any scenes when you ride off into the sunset."

He looked down at her. "Suddenly you know the future?"

Chuckling wryly, she murmured, "I think pretty much any woman could tell what you're thinking now."

Looking annoyed, he shrugged into his shirt. "That's bull."

"Maybe."

"So *you're* not having second thoughts?"

"Second. Third. Fourth."

Her dry repetition seemed to ease some of his tension. He paused by the side of the bed. "Sorry. I guess I've just had a lot to process today."

"I know. It's been a long day for both of us."

He leaned over to brush a surprisingly

gentle kiss against her lips. "I'll see you in the morning."

"All right. Sleep well."

He paused again at the door, one hand on the knob. "Aislinn?"

"Yes?"

"No matter what happens, I'm not really sorry."

She smiled. "Neither am I. No matter what."

He let himself out the door, closing it firmly behind him.

Aislinn fell back against the pillows. Okay, maybe that had been a mistake. And she was well aware that she was the one who had initiated it, though Ethan had certainly been a willing participant. And maybe her heart was going to be bruised, if not broken, before this rather quixotic quest was over.

But whatever happened, she wasn't sorry. For once, she had done something bold, reckless, a little wild—and while she had no intention of radically changing the quiet, rather conservative life she had led to this point, it had felt good to step out of her rut for just this one night. Amazing, actually.

Maybe there was a tiny bit of her mother in her, after all.

Chapter Thirteen

"Little Ethan Brannon. I can't believe it."

Ethan forced a smile, though he was more tempted to grimace.

Eighty-year-old Odessa Hester folded her hands across her large stomach and beamed at him and Aislinn as they sat side by side on the afghan-draped and pillow-crowded sofa in her overfurnished living room. There was barely room for their knees between the sofa and the knickknack-covered coffee table. The big recliner that supported Odessa's substantial weight was wedged between another table and a three-light floor lamp.

The smallish room also held an entertainment center with a medium-size television set, two packed-full curio cabinets, a wing chair, a rocking chair and a large leather ottoman. Every flat surface was covered in bric-a-brac, most of it of the inexpensive, dollar-store variety, but there wasn't a speck of dust in sight.

He vaguely remembered this house. Every room was like this one, filled almost to bulging with furniture and decorations. When he was little, he'd found it fascinating, with so many things to see, so many nooks and crannies to explore. Odessa had happily invited him and his brothers to explore as much as they wanted. To make it more fun, she'd hidden candy and small toys before they'd arrived to keep them entertained while she and his mother visited. Funny how he'd forgotten that until today.

"How is your dear mother, Ethan?"

"She's fine, thank you, Mrs. Hester."

"Oh, honey, you might as well call me Odessa now. Everyone does. Are you sure I can't get either of you some pie? A soda?"

Both he and Aislinn politely declined. He could tell Aislinn was captivated by the large, friendly woman in the colorful clothing.

"So tell me why you're here, Ethan. Are you showing your girlfriend where you lived when you were a little boy?"

He didn't bother to correct her about Aislinn's identity, though the term made him vaguely uncomfortable. "Something like that," he said instead. "I haven't been back here since we moved away, you know."

His former next-door neighbor sighed lightly. "I know. I'd hoped your folks would come back to visit sometimes, but I guess it was just too painful for them, bless their hearts."

"They've made a good life for themselves in Alabama," he assured her. "Dad stays busy in his orthodontics office and Mom's involved in a half dozen charities, of course."

"She always did love to stay involved in the community."

"Still does."

"And your brother? How's Joel doing? I know he's a doctor, because your mother still sends me a Christmas card every year and tells me family news. He lives in Arkansas, doesn't he?"

"That's right. Did you know he got married again two weeks ago?"

"No, I didn't. Good for him. Do you like your new sister-in-law?"

"Very much," he said sincerely. "I think she and Joel will be happy."

"That's nice to hear. Your family's suffered enough loss. It's time for you all to be happy." She beamed at Aislinn, who squirmed a bit self-consciously on the couch. "How long have you known Ethan, hon?"

"Not very long," Aislinn replied. "I met him through Joel's new wife, Nic, who's been my best friend for years."

"Well, isn't that nice? Do I hear more wedding bells in store for the Brannon family? You aren't getting any younger, you know, Ethan. What are you? Thirty-three? Thirty-four now?"

Tempted to squirm himself, Ethan said lightly, "I'm thirty-six. I'll turn thirty-seven in a few weeks."

"Thirty-six," she repeated with a slow shake of her head. "Can you imagine that? I'll have to tell Vic when he gets home from visiting his brother out at the nursing home. He'll be sorry he missed you. He always thought the world of your dad, you know."

Ethan barely remembered Odessa's husband. He had a faint memory of a large, quiet man who always carried sticks of gum that he liked to hand out to the neighborhood kids. Odessa and Vic had never had children of their own, but they'd taken pleasure in being honorary aunt and uncle to dozens.

More than ready to change the subject, Ethan

got to the point of their drop-in visit. "Odessa, do you remember Carmen Nichols?"

"The nanny who died with poor little Kyle? Of course I remember her. She used to have coffee with me sometimes while Kyle took his nap. Nice woman, if a little reserved."

"Reserved in what way?"

"Oh, you know. Didn't talk about herself much. Wouldn't really share details about her life. She'd talk about you kids and about movies and television programs she enjoyed, books she'd read, that sort of thing.... But getting her to talk about herself was like pulling teeth."

"So you don't really know anything about her."

"Well, you know I'm pretty good at drawing people out. I learned a few things."

Sitting up straighter, he asked, "Like what?"

"Mind if I ask why you want to know?"

"Aislinn and I are looking into the accident," he said candidly. "My family still has a lot of questions about exactly what happened that day, and I decided it's past time one of us tried to find some answers. Like why Carmen took Kyle out that day and where she was going when she left the house with him."

"I don't blame you for wondering," Odessa said with a sigh. "I've asked myself those same questions many times during the past thirty years."

"You were the one who saw her leave the house that afternoon, weren't you?"

Odessa nodded. "I was looking out to see if the rain was letting up. I saw her putting Kyle in the toddler seat she kept in her car for him. Never was a very good seat," she added with a shake of her head. "But she didn't take him out very often, so your mama wasn't too worried about it, though I know she planned to buy a new one when she got the chance."

"Did Carmen see you watching her? Did she look upset or anxious?"

"I don't know if she saw me. I don't think so. I was too far away to see her expression, exactly. And she had a hood over her head to protect her from the rain. One of those yellow slicker-type raincoats. She was very fond of that coat. She wore it every time it even drizzled a little. Your daddy used to tease her about it, call it her banana coat."

"You said you drew a little out of her about her private life. Can you remember anything in particular?"

Odessa waved her pudgy hands in a vague gesture. "She told me she'd married young but that he'd died. She said she'd grown up in Mississippi but that she was an orphan."

Ethan frowned. "Mississippi? Not Florida?"

"No, I'm pretty sure it was Mississippi."

"She told my mother she was from Florida and that her family disowned her when she married."

"That's odd. It's not at all the story she told me."

"Did she have any special friends around here? Anyone she dated or just hung out with?"

Odessa nodded. "There was one woman about her age. They used to go to movies and stuff together. Sometimes the other girl would come over to your house while your mama was off volunteering, and she and Carmen would watch soap operas together in the afternoon."

"Do you remember her name? Do you know if she's still in this area?"

"Oh, yes, I still see her occasionally. She works over at the Kroger store on Maple Street. Her name is Natalie, but I can't recall her last name, if I ever knew it."

"That's fine. You've given us quite a bit as it is."

"I wish I could tell you more. I can understand why you'd be struggling with this. It has bothered me for thirty years that I didn't try to ask Carmen where she was going on such a stormy day."

"No one would have expected you to do so, Odessa. Just one more question, if I may. Does the name Mark mean anything to you in connection with Carmen?"

Aislinn looked at him thoughtfully while Odessa gave the question a moment's consideration. And then Odessa shook her head. "Not that I know of."

Ethan couldn't think of anything else to ask. Though he was impatient to move on, it took another twenty minutes for them to take their leave of Odessa. She wanted to reminisce a bit more about the years when his family had lived next door, and Ethan didn't want to be rude when she was being so nice and helpful.

"Thought we were never going to get out of there," he said when he and Aislinn were on their way.

"Mmm. She was nice."

She sounded distracted, distant. She'd been rather quiet all morning—and he supposed he couldn't blame her for that, considering the way he'd run out on her last night, but this was different. He was beginning to recognize this tone.

"What did you pick up in there?" he asked.

"Carmen wasn't from Mississippi. Not from Florida, either."

"So where was she from?"

"I'm not sure. But it was somewhere in the South," she suggested tentatively.

"Have you ever figured out what connection the state of Georgia has to all of this? Do you think that's where Kyle is now?"

"Maybe."

"You're full of maybes today."

"Sorry. It's the best I can do."

"It does seem suspicious that Carmen told my mother and Odessa different stories about her past," he conceded. That was hardly proof that she had snatched his brother, of course, he reminded himself.

He didn't have to express his lingering reservations. Aislinn merely nodded. "She had a lot to hide."

"Did you sense anything else while we were talking to Odessa?"

Her face was somber when she nodded.

"Only that it's a good thing you had a chance to visit with her today. You'll appreciate that memory soon."

Startled, he tightened his hands on the steering wheel. "You think she's ill?"

"Very ill."

"Should we go back and tell her? Maybe she should go to the doctor...."

"She knows, Ethan."

He reminded himself that Aislinn could be wrong. He still wasn't ready to accept everything she said as fact. But still, he was glad now that he'd spent that extra twenty minutes with Odessa.

"Of course I remember Carmen. She was the best friend I ever had."

Natalie Mitchell's pale blue eyes filled with tears as she spoke, and she dabbed at them with the back of one weathered hand. A hard-lived sixty, Natalie had once been a redhead, though her hair was mostly gray now. She had probably never been pretty, but the face they saw now was the victim of too much sun and too many frowns.

They'd found Natalie at her home, after being told by one of her coworkers that she wasn't working that day. The coworker had given them her last name, and Ethan had found her address in a local telephone book. More trusting than she should have been, she had let them into her rented duplex when they'd told her that they were there to ask about Carmen.

"Who did you say you are?"

"Ethan Brannon," he told her. "My brother was with Carmen the day she…died."

If Natalie noticed the slight hesitation, she didn't react. Aislinn, however, had noted it.

Natalie swiped at her eyes again. "You were the oldest," she murmured. "I remember you. I used to come over to your house to visit Carmen sometimes. Don't you remember?"

Sitting in one of two undersize armchairs in the shabby living room while Aislinn sat in the other and Natalie on the couch, Ethan shook his head. "No, I'm afraid not."

"Well, you were little. And, come to think of it, you were already in school. Joel was in kindergarten. I'd come over while the baby was asleep and me and Carmen would watch TV and sometimes play cards."

Aislinn studied the woman, picking up no trace of deception in her. Sadness, yes. Regrets, definitely. But there seemed to be no doubt that Natalie believed her friend had died when everyone else thought she did.

"I'm simply trying to understand exactly what happened that day," Ethan explained to her.

Natalie sighed heavily. "If you knew how many times I've asked myself that same question…"

"Can you tell me about Carmen? I don't remember her very well. I remember that she was quiet."

"She was a little quiet around people she didn't know very well," Natalie agreed. "But once you got to know her, she was a lot of fun. We used to laugh over those card games...." She sighed again as the words trailed off.

"Did she talk to you much about her past?"

"Neither one of us wanted to talk much about our pasts," Natalie muttered. "Mine hadn't been so great, and she told me hers wasn't, either."

"Did she say where she grew up? I've heard Florida—or maybe Mississippi."

Natalie frowned and slowly shook her head. "She just said she moved around a lot when she was growing up. She didn't claim any particular state that I recall."

"What about boyfriends? Did she date? Do you remember a guy named Mark?"

"I don't remember anyone named Mark. Carmen didn't date much. She didn't meet many men working at the day-care center where I met her. Nor sitting there with you kids. After work, she tended to go straight home and watch a lot of TV. I didn't date much, either," she added. "Not for lack of wanting to. I just rarely met anyone who was interested in going out with me."

Aislinn sensed that there was something more. "So she wasn't seeing anyone before she disappeared?"

Natalie hesitated, then said reluctantly, "Maybe someone in the weeks before. There were several nights when I asked her if she wanted to do something and she told me she had other plans. It hurt my feelings that she wouldn't tell me more. Up until then, I thought we told each other everything."

Someone had picked Carmen up on that highway that afternoon, Aislinn mused. Someone who had agreed ahead of time to meet her there and help her spirit away the child in her care. She didn't know who it had been, whether man or woman, but it hadn't been Natalie.

"You've been very generous with your time," Ethan said, standing, which signaled Aislinn to rise to her feet, as well. "Just one more question, if I may, and I'm afraid it's going to sound strange."

Rising, Natalie looked at him questioningly. "What is it?"

"Do you think there's any possibility that Carmen didn't die that day? That she chose to simply disappear instead, taking my brother with her?"

Aislinn was startled to hear him so bluntly sum up her theory of what had happened that day. This was the first time he had even suggested to anyone else that there was a possibility Carmen had survived.

Natalie had started shaking her head before Ethan even finished asking the question. "I don't know where you got that idea, but it's crazy," she said flatly. "Carmen was happy here. There was no reason at all for her to do anything like that."

Holding up a hand in a conciliatory gesture, Ethan spoke soothingly. "I didn't say it did happen that way. I was just asking. You can probably understand that I've always looked for reasons to hope that my brother would be returned to the family someday, and since the bodies were never found…"

Calming a little, Natalie nodded. "I can see why you wouldn't want to give up hope. I felt the same way for a long time after Carmen disappeared. I missed her so much, you see. She was the only real friend I had back then. And it bothered me to know she would never have a proper burial, never have a place where I could take flowers every so often and, you know, sort of talk to her.

"So every weekend for the next year I'd go out and drive along the river, as far down as I could imagine the flood carrying her. Sometimes I'd get out and walk the banks, looking for something, anything, that would give me a clue of what happened to her. I thought the authorities gave up too soon, you see. I wanted them to keep looking, even after they called off the search. And then one day I found proof that Carmen had been washed downstream, several miles from where the car went over the side."

Aislinn and Ethan exchanged a startled look.

"You found proof?" Ethan asked.

Natalie nodded. "Wait here."

She disappeared into the back of her home, then rejoined them carrying an old-looking, square cardboard box. She set the box on the table, lifted the lid and carefully drew out a tattered, stained strip of once-yellow weather-ized fabric.

"This was a piece of the coat she was wearing that day," she murmured, stroking it gently with one hand. "I found it wedged under a rock along the riverbank. There was a lot of other debris from the flood in that area, too, at a place where the river is really wide and deep. I figured the stuff was deposited there as the water receded and that Carmen's body was probably trapped under more rubble some-where underwater. I go there now every year on the anniversary of her death and throw flowers in the water. It makes me feel like she has a burial place after all."

Ethan was obviously shaken by the revelation, but his voice was steady when he asked, "How do you know this was a piece of her coat? It's just a scrap of cloth."

Natalie turned the fabric to reveal the other side. "Her initials are embroidered on it. See? C.N. She did this herself one day while I was visiting her. This was her coat, Ethan. I guess it was ripped off her in the flood, then shredded by debris. It's one of the few things I have left of her."

"Do you know what became of her belongings?" Aislinn asked, one of the first questions she had asked of the woman.

"There weren't that many. Since she didn't have family, the things she'd left at her apartment were sold to pay off her bills. She didn't have a life insurance policy, nor a will. Whatever was left over was donated to charity, I believe."

"Do you mind if I touch that fabric?"

Though she looked surprised, Natalie shrugged. "I suppose not."

Aislinn sensed Ethan watching her closely as she placed her hand on the torn cloth. A moment later she dropped her hand. "Thank you."

"You're welcome, I guess." Natalie folded the fabric back into the box. "Is there anything else you want to know?"

Shaking his head, Ethan put a hand on Aislinn's arm and nudged her toward the door. "That's all, thanks."

She saw them out with polite bemusement.

Sitting across a restaurant table from Ethan, Aislinn watched him pick at his plate of spaghetti without much evidence of either appetite or pleasure. His thoughts were obviously far away.

It was early for dinner, but he hadn't seemed to know what else to suggest when they'd left Natalie's place. He'd said he was hungry, but the way he acted now proved that hadn't been true. She knew he'd needed time to think about what they had learned today and something to occupy his hands while he did so.

Having ordered a chef's salad for herself, she poked her fork into a plump cherry tomato and asked, "What's our next step?"

He looked up from his plate, fully meeting her eyes for the first time since they'd left Natalie. "I don't know about you, but I think I'll head back to Danston in the morning. I have work that needs to be done there, and I'm pretty sure I'd be wasting my time staying here any longer."

"What about the search for your brother?"

He set down his fork, giving up all pretense of eating. "Isn't it obvious that we've reached a dead end? We've talked to everyone we can find who even remembers Carmen from thirty years ago. There isn't a shred of evidence that she didn't go over the side of that road. We don't know where she lived before she came here, don't even know for certain that Carmen

Nichols was her real name. Though I can't imagine why she'd have lied about that."

"You're starting to doubt me again, aren't you?"

"I have always doubted you," he reminded her. "Not your motives, necessarily. You seem to believe the things you say. But as for their accuracy—"

"You think I'm making it all up."

"I didn't say that, either. Don't put words in my mouth. I'd be a fool to deny that you have some special gifts. An ability to sense some things that most people can't. I don't think you're crazy or unnatural or any of the things your grandfather obsessed about. Maybe it's like you've always said, just heightened intuition or a real talent for guessing things. But this time I think maybe you let yourself get carried away."

"Carried away," she repeated, pushing her salad bowl aside. "You're suggesting that I've concocted this whole tale about Carmen faking her death and disappearing with Kyle."

"Not intentionally," he assured her.

"That's supposed to appease me?"

"I'm not trying to appease you," he said crossly. "I'm just trying to be honest."

"And you honestly think I'm wrong about what happened to Carmen and Kyle."

He sighed and pushed a hand through his hair. "I have to repeat, there's no evidence at all that they're still alive. We have a witness who saw her get in her car with Kyle and who saw her wearing the yellow coat that Natalie found months later, far downriver from where the car went in. Though we never found her, there was a witness who called the police and reported the car going over. There were certainly some inconsistencies with the stories Carmen told about her background, but it's a big leap from a few fibs to kidnapping."

"Kyle is alive, Ethan," she said wearily, knowing she had already lost.

"Then tell me where he is."

"I wish I could."

"You touched Carmen's coat. Did you get anything from it about what really happened that day? Where she is now if not in the river?"

"No. I didn't get anything. I didn't expect to, really, but I thought it was worth a try."

"So there's nothing more we can do, is there? Unless you get some sort of vision that leads straight to Kyle, it looks like you and I have done all we can."

But he didn't expect that to happen, she thought sadly. Because he had closed his mind to the possibility that she might be right.

As they drove in silence back to the motel, she thought about his turnaround. She knew he had been on the verge of believing. That she had almost convinced him she could be trusted.

But then they had made the mistake of getting too close—and in his self-protective retreat, Ethan had looked for any excuse he could find to pull away. For some reason, that scrap of yellow cloth had provided all the proof he needed to put an end to this uncomfortable journey.

He walked her to her door but made no move to enter. "I'm going to make arrangements for a flight home in the morning. I assume you'll want to do the same."

She nodded, hearing defeat in her voice when she said, "Fine."

"I'm planning to spend the evening in my room, catching up on some computer work."

"Yes, I'll do the same."

"Let me know what time you need to be at the airport. We'll want to get an early start."

"I'll call you as soon as I have a time."

"Good." He hesitated a moment longer. "You probably shouldn't swim after the pool closes tonight. It really isn't safe for you to be out alone like that."

"I won't be swimming tonight."

He nodded and turned away. "Good night, Aislinn," he said without looking back at her.

"Goodbye, Ethan," she whispered as she closed herself into her room.

* * *

Aislinn's plane was scheduled to leave before Ethan's, and their gates were at opposite ends of the airport. "There's no need for you to stay here with me," she told him after he walked her to hers. "I have a book in my bag."

"Are you sure?"

"I'm sure. It's only going to be an hour, and I've been trying to find time to finish this book for weeks."

He looked almost relieved, which didn't do a lot for her ego. "I guess I'll leave you to your reading then."

"All right." She held out her hand. "Have a safe flight, Ethan."

He looked at her hand a moment before taking it. And then he spoke impulsively. "Look, I'm sorry, okay? I guess there was a part of me that really wanted to believe you."

She drew her hand from his. "And another part of you that never wanted to even try."

"You can't say I didn't give it a shot," he

said, sounding defensive. "I came here with you, didn't I? I spent the whole day yesterday talking to strangers, pretty much making a fool of myself."

"I didn't force you to do that. It was always up to you whether you wanted to act on the information I gave you."

"And I acted. But you still seem to be disappointed that I'm ending the search. What else would you have me do, Aislinn?"

"I'm not sure. Maybe try to find employment records or tax records or something to trace Carmen's background, which might give us a clue where she went."

"That would be a major undertaking, even if we could find anything useful. I don't have that kind of time to spend on what would probably turn out to be a futile exercise. You don't, either. You have a business to run. Orders to fill."

"I'm aware of my responsibilities to my clients," she said coolly.

"So go back to them. I appreciate your effort to help my family, but in the long run, maybe it's better this way."

"Better?"

"I don't believe Kyle's out there, okay? But if he is, maybe he's perfectly happy. Maybe he's got a great life and we'd just be messing it up by tracking him down. Maybe he wouldn't want a new family. For that matter, my family's doing pretty well right now. Mom and Dad are healthy and content, Joel's a blissful newlywed, I'm satisfied with my life. Why risk upsetting everyone again?"

She was stunned by his seemingly careless words. "Are you saying that if I could give you definitive information on how to find Kyle, you would turn your back on him? Because it would be easier to pretend none of this ever happened?"

They stood in a relatively private spot in the busy terminal in a back corner of the waiting area. Still, Aislinn was aware of a few curious looks as passing strangers sensed the tension between them. She didn't care.

"You really think I don't know why you've been such a loner the past few years, Ethan?" she continued in a low voice. "Why you avoid people except in the line of business? Why you live in your isolated river cabin where no one but family ever visits you?"

"You don't know me at all," he growled. "No matter what you think you might sense about me."

"I know you've been hurt. Disappointed. Betrayed. You've lost people you loved, you've loved people you shouldn't have. And now you protect yourself. Too well, maybe."

He moved a step backward. "You're really reaching now."

"Am I? Because I think you're afraid, Ethan. I think you're afraid to start believing Kyle might still be out there. Because you think it would hurt too much if you found out later that you were wrong."

"I don't—"

But she didn't give him a chance to finish the denial. "It all comes down to me, doesn't it? Whether you can trust me. And trust is something you don't give anyone anymore.

"You're afraid," she said again. "Afraid that if you did start to trust me, you could end up disillusioned if it turns out that I really have been playing you for a fool. Afraid that I see too much when I look at you, more than you let most people see. Afraid of getting your heart broken again. That's why you don't trust me to get near it."

His brows were drawn downward into a fierce frown. "You don't know what you're talking about."

"I know you were in love with Heather. And that the night she married your brother, you told yourself you would never open your heart like that again. And you haven't. Whenever anyone gets too close, you run. Just like you're running now."

The words had left her before she could stop them. Maybe because she knew this was her one last chance to convince him that she understood his fears. And that he should believe what she told him.

But she had gone too far. His face white, Ethan took another step away from her. "Goodbye, Aislinn. Have a safe trip home," he said, his voice harsh.

Conceding defeat, she nodded. "I will. And so will you."

He ignored the dry prediction as he turned. And then he paused and glanced back over his shoulder. "Like I said, I don't believe it will ever become an option. But for the record, no, I wouldn't turn my back on my brother."

"And yet that's exactly what you're doing," she whispered.

He spun without another word and walked away. Effectively turning his back on both of them.

Chapter Fourteen

"I'm glad to hear you've been sleeping better, Cassandra."

"Yes, it's been much better. Thank you, Dr. Thomas."

He glanced at the sweater folded neatly on the end of her bed. "It looks like you've completed your project."

"Yes." Her hands felt empty without the knitting needles, but she knew she would never hold them again. "I finished yesterday."

"It's great. A beautiful color."

"Thank you."

"I suppose you'll be starting a new one soon."

"Mmm." Because she didn't want to talk about that now, she changed the subject. "You've been very good to me, Dr. Thomas. I'm going to miss you."

He went still, then asked cautiously, "Are you going somewhere?"

Smiling indulgently at him, she replied, "No. I'll be staying here. You're the one who's leaving, aren't you?"

"I, um, what do you mean?"

"Now, Dr. Thomas, don't be evasive. I know you're making a career change. And I don't want to spend our last few days together pretending ignorance."

He shook his head. "How could you possibly know I've accepted a partnership in a new clinic? I haven't told anyone here yet."

"I have my ways of knowing things," she replied with a faint smile.

He looked at her, sitting by the window in her

wheelchair, and then at the closed door through which so few people ever entered. "Has anyone ever told you you're a little scary, Cassandra?"

"All the time," she assured him. "So when will you be leaving?"

Sighing in resignation, he replied, "At the end of the month. I had planned to make the announcement early next week."

"You can still do so. I haven't mentioned it to anyone else."

"I'll miss everyone here, you know."

"I know. But you're making the right move. Your life is going to change a great deal in the next year. It's going to be stressful for you at first, as change always is, but everything will work out fine. You're going to have a good life and you deserve it. You're a fine young man."

"And you know all of this…how?"

"Let's just say I have certain talents and leave it at that, shall we?"

He cleared his throat, obviously uncomfortable. But she was used to that. There was a great deal more she could tell him about the changes awaiting him, but she thought she'd better stop now. He would have to find his own way in his future, and she knew he would do so, though not without difficulty. But then, life wasn't meant to be entirely easy, was it?

"I think you have a lot of talents, Cassandra. I'm not sure predicting the future is one of them," he added with a faint smile, "but I'm not ruling it out, either. I've never met anyone quite like you. Would you mind if I come visit you sometimes after I leave?"

"I would be delighted to see you. Anytime," she assured him, though she suspected there was a sad edge to her smile.

"Is there anything else I can do for you before I go today?"

"As a matter of fact, there is. See that envelope on my nightstand?"

He picked up the envelope and glanced automatically at the front. "This one?"

"Yes. I'm afraid I don't have any stamps. Would you mind mailing that for me?"

She knew he was a little curious about why she'd asked him rather than a member of the staff, but he merely nodded. "I'd be happy to. Don't you want to put a return address on it first?"

"No, it's fine, thank you." She didn't add that the reason she had asked him to mail it was because she knew he would do so from a post office near his home, which was in a different city than the residential facility where she lived.

"Well, I'll see you tomorrow then. I'd better go now and check to see how Mrs. Campbell is settling in. She's the new resident two rooms down. Have you met her yet? She seems nice."

"No, I haven't met her." Mrs. Kennedy had occupied that room until recently, when she had died rather unexpectedly. It had happened the day the staff had encountered so much trouble waking Cassandra and had called Dr. Thomas as a result.

"Maybe you should join some of the activities this afternoon. You might just surprise yourself and make some friends."

He was still worried that she was lonely, she thought after he let himself out. He couldn't know that she was most content when she was alone these days. Which didn't mean the same applied to him. It would be good for him to have new people in his life. But she would miss him.

The plastic line on the gasoline-powered weed trimmer sliced through the grass that had grown high around the concrete pad of the cedar-shake-topped gazebo in Ethan's backyard. Cuttings flew through the air, sticking to his jeans and boots. Sweat dripped from his hair and from beneath his protective goggles. Trimming was his least favorite part of yard work, but it was the price he paid to keep his place looking good. Strictly for himself.

Moving on to trim around the stone barbecue, he thought about the raspberry iced tea that waited in the refrigerator. The cold beverage was going to taste great after all this manual labor in the heat of the summer afternoon.

He pictured himself sprawled in one of the rockers on the deck, sipping tea and watching the river roll by. There was nothing he'd rather be doing. No company he'd rather have than his own.

At least that was what he had always believed.

He'd never been lonely here before. Never regretted his choice to live a rather solitary existence in his rural refuge. Never entertained the thought that he had done so out of fear rather than simple preference. Until Aislinn had made him start to question himself.

It wasn't fear, he assured himself now, angrily attacking a new patch of weeds. He was no coward. So maybe he'd suffered some losses in his life. Maybe his heart had been bruised a time or two. Maybe he had loved unwisely once or twice. Didn't mean those experiences had left him afraid. Just cautious. Maybe a little hardened.

On the rare occasions when the thought of settling down with someone had crossed his mind during the past few years, he'd always assured himself that he was fine on his own. He was too obstinate to be married, too set in his ways. Too jaded to fall in love again now. He'd long since stopped believing in fantasy or magic. Until Aislinn had told him things no one else could have known and made him start questioning everything he had believed before.

He had accused her once of hypnotizing him, he remembered, staring out at the river for a moment, the machine still chugging in his hands. He wondered now if she really had. How else could he explain the fact that she still haunted him two weeks after he had walked away from her? Two long, restless weeks since he'd told himself she came with too many complications and too many strings to make it worth pursuing anything with her?

What else could account for the way he kept seeing her, even here in his home where she'd never stepped foot? In his bed, where she had visited only in fevered dreams?

What else could make him still want to go to her now despite the acrimonious way they had parted? He had been furious with her when he'd stalked away from her, dismayed that she guessed things about him that he'd thought he'd hidden deeply away from everyone. Including himself.

And yet he'd spent the past week trying to talk himself out of contacting her again. He had even considered resuming the search for the brother he didn't believe was out there, just because it would provide another excuse to see Aislinn again.

He'd known he was in trouble when he had started trying to convince himself that being with Aislinn again would be a smart move.

That spending more time with her would let him work her out of his system in a way. That his lingering fascination with her would surely fade away with familiarity.

It had been lust, plain and simple, he told himself. And that was something that faded rather quickly, in his experience. So maybe it felt different this time with Aislinn. But then, Aislinn was very different from the women he had known before.

Silencing the noisy trimmer, he pushed the goggles to the top of his head and turned, grimly trying to think about anything but Aislinn. When he saw her standing on the pathway behind him, he thought at first that he was being haunted by another memory of her.

And then she spoke. "Hello, Ethan."

She looked as beautiful as ever, if a bit pale. Her dark, wavy hair was loose around her face and shoulders, her body very straight and rather tense in a cream-colored top and brown slacks. She gripped a crumpled envelope in her hands so tightly her knuckles were white around it.

Very conscious of his sweat and dishevelment, the dirt and grass stains on his torn T-shirt, jeans and old boots, he asked more gruffly than he'd intended, "What are you doing here?"

"I know I should have called," she said apologetically. "But I had to talk to you and I didn't want to do it over the phone."

He figured she must have thought it was important or she wouldn't have come all this way. Which meant it probably wasn't going to be a quick conversation.

"Let me clean up first," he said, not liking the feeling that he was at a disadvantage. "You can have a glass of tea or something while I shower. Then we'll talk."

She didn't attempt to argue with him.

By the time he had showered and changed into a clean shirt and jeans, he felt a bit more in control of his emotions. Aislinn might have caught him off guard, showing up without warning as she had, but he was ready now to deal with her. At least he hoped so, he thought as she looked up at him with an uncharacteristic vulnerability that tugged at his hardened heart.

She started to stand, but he waved her back onto the sofa where he'd left her with a glass of tea when he'd gone to shower. Like her, he had furnished his home for comfort, with deep, over-stuffed furniture, functional tables and built-in shelving for books and entertainment equipment. A stone fireplace dominated the living room, and in the winter there was usually a warm fire crackling there. Glass doors at the back of the room provided a view of his deck, picnic pavilion, private boat dock and the river beyond.

He had put a great deal of himself into this house and its furnishings. He doubted that Aislinn had missed a thing during the short time she'd been alone in here.

"You want any more tea?" he asked, moving

past her toward the sunny, eat-in kitchen with its industrial appliances.

"No, thank you."

He poured himself a glass, then carried it back into the living room and sat in a chair across from her. He didn't quite trust himself to sit on the couch beside her. "Okay," he said after taking a long swallow of his tea. "I'm ready."

She laced her fingers in her lap. "First, I want to apologize for the way we parted at the airport," she said. "I was out of line and I'm sorry."

He shrugged, not wanting to discuss the details of what she had said. "We were both mad and frustrated by the dead ends we'd hit," he said. "Forget it. That wasn't the only reason you came, was it?"

She shook her head.

"Have you come up with more details about Kyle?" he asked, wondering what he would do if she had. He should tell her he wasn't interested in any more wild-goose chasing. If he was smart, he would keep his distance from her from now on, hoping his unwelcome fascination with her would fade in time. But he would still listen to what she had come to say.

She smoothed the white envelope she had been holding since she'd arrived, but she didn't open it just then. "Since I got home, I've been working very hard, trying to put your family issues out of my mind," she admitted. "You didn't want me to tell anyone else about what I believed happened to Kyle, and I had no way to prove any of it. Like you said, we had hit a dead end. And I was still upset over the way we separated, so it just seemed easier not to think about it."

He knew that feeling. He wondered if she had been any more successful than he at blocking the memories. Something told him she hadn't. "So you haven't learned anything new?"

"Not—not on my own."

"What does that mean?"

She held out the envelope then. "This was in my mail two days ago. I don't know who sent it."

Looking into her troubled eyes, he took the envelope from her and opened it, taking out a single sheet of paper. Unfolding it, he frowned when he saw the drawing. He recognized the face. It was the same one Aislinn had supposedly drawn in her sleep. Though the pose was different, the style was almost identical. He would have sworn they had been drawn by the same hand.

He still wasn't sure they hadn't, he thought, looking up at her slowly.

"I didn't draw this one," she insisted, obviously reading his thoughts in his expression. "It came in the mail. No return address. Post-marked Atlanta, Georgia."

He looked at it again. The face that she had told him was his brother. He'd looked at the drawing she'd given him a dozen times since he'd returned home, and there were very few differences between the two.

This wasn't what he had expected at all. He'd thought maybe she would tell him some more details about the accident or more vague clues about where Carmen had supposedly taken Kyle. But this, if he were to believe her, made everything even more strange and unsettling than anything she had told him yet.

"Look at the back," she urged, her voice strangely flat, uninflected.

He turned the sheet over. There was a name written in small block print. *Dr. Mark Thomas.* And an address below it, located in Georgia.

"Mark," he said, the significance of the name hitting him then.

Aislinn nodded.

"And you don't know who sent you this."

"I—no."

He sighed impatiently.

"I don't," she said defensively. "But when I held it, I thought I should know, for some reason. That's the best I can do to explain it."

He set the drawing aside and stood, moving

to look out the window. He felt strangely as if his entire future hinged on however he handled the next few minutes—and he wasn't sure if he was ready for this at all.

As she'd said, he didn't give his trust easily. And what she was asking him to believe now required a leap of faith greater than any he had ever taken before.

Still sitting on the couch, Aislinn studied Ethan's back, giving him time to process what she had told him. She knew how difficult this must be for him. It had been one of the hardest things she'd ever done to come here at all.

She remembered the impact of seeing that drawing that had arrived in her mail. It had hit her with such a physical force that she'd staggered, almost falling into a chair. She still couldn't look at it without a chill running down her spine.

It had been the truth when she'd told Ethan she didn't know who sent it to her. But every time she touched it, she got a...feeling. A nagging whisper at the back of her mind that she should know. That she wasn't letting herself know.

After another moment, she stood and moved closer to Ethan, stopping a few steps away. "Ethan?"

"You must realize how this sounds."

"Trust me, I know. I was aware of how hard it would be for you to believe me when I came. I tried to talk myself out of coming, since you'd made it clear you wanted to stop searching. But I knew I had to tell you about this."

He turned then to look at her. "It would be easy for me to believe that you're trying to put something over on me. That you're playing with my mind. That you drew both those pictures and that you've made up this whole bizarre tale, for some reason."

"I can see why it would be reasonable for you to think that," she agreed evenly. "All I can tell you is that you would be wrong. Everything I've said to you happened exactly the way I told you it did. I drew the first picture I showed you. Someone else drew this one. Someone who then mailed it to me, along with the name and address on the back."

"And you think that name is the one my brother is using now."

She nodded. "I know it is. Dr. Mark Thomas is your brother, Kyle."

He moved a step closer to her and cupped her face between his hands, looking deeply into her eyes. "Tell me one more time."

Though her pulse raced in response to his touch, her voice was steady when she said, "I'm telling you the truth, Ethan. And despite how improbable this all sounds, I'm asking you to trust me."

His gaze traveled from her eyes to her mouth and then back again. She held her breath while he made up his mind, taking so long that she was beginning to get a little light-headed by the time he finally dropped his hands and stepped away.

"All right," he said brusquely. "I'll throw some things in a bag."

She breathed deeply, then let it out on a slow, unsteady exhale. "We're going to Georgia?"

"We're going to Georgia."

For some reason, Aislinn had thought the address on the back of the drawing might be an office. Maybe because of the title before the name. Instead she and Ethan found themselves in a residential neighborhood of nice, tasteful brick homes. A young-professionals neighborhood, she thought, filled with couples on the rise in their careers.

It hadn't occurred to her that Kyle could be married now or have children. He would be thirty-two, certainly old enough—and yet she had the feeling that he was still single, despite the family-style house.

Sitting behind the wheel of the rental car, Ethan studied the windows of the house. It was early evening, not dark yet, so it was hard to tell if the lights were on inside. But Aislinn sensed that Kyle—or Mark, as he was known now—was home. Blissfully unaware that his life was about to change drastically.

"This is nuts," Ethan grumbled beneath his breath, sounding a little nervous.

"Maybe," she agreed. "But we have to do this."

He turned in the seat to look at her. "You're asking me to take a huge step here. To risk making a complete fool of myself."

"I know."

His eyes grave, he murmured, "I wouldn't have done this for anyone but you."

She let the meaning of that sink in. Ethan was telling her that he trusted her. And that hadn't been an easy admission for him.

"Thank you," she said unsteadily.

"Okay." Dragging his gaze from hers, he reached for his door handle. "Let's do this."

They walked side by side to the front door of the Georgian-style house. There they paused and looked at each other again. After a moment, Ethan held out his left hand. Swallowing hard, Aislinn put her right hand in his palm, feeling his fingers close around hers. And then he pushed the doorbell.

The door opened a few moments later. Aislinn stared at the nice-looking man who stood just inside the house. There was a definite family resemblance, she noted, though Ethan and Joel looked more like each other. But she had no doubt he was their brother.

"May I help you?" he asked, looking from Ethan to her and back again.

"Dr. Mark Thomas?" Ethan asked.

"Yes."

"I'm Ethan Brannon. This is Aislinn Flaherty."

"Nice to meet you." The way his voice rose a little at the end turned it into a question.

Ethan glanced at Aislinn again, then, when she nodded slightly, looked back at the other man. "This is going to sound strange, I know, but I hope you'll give us a chance to explain. There's a, um…there's a chance that you and I could be brothers."

Mark Thomas looked hard at Ethan for a moment and then he took a step backward. "I think you'd better come inside."

Chapter Fifteen

At least he hadn't thrown them out, Aislinn thought a half hour later, after she and Ethan had told Dr. Mark Thomas everything that had led them to him. To be honest, they'd made such a mess of it that she was rather surprised he hadn't called the authorities.

"So let me get this straight," he repeated slowly, the first time he had spoken in a while. "You—" he looked at Aislinn "—are a little bit psychic. And you got the feeling that Ethan's brother was kidnapped thirty years ago."

Trying not to grimace at the way he made it sound, she nodded.

"And you—" Mark turned to Ethan "—aren't sure you believe in psychics, but because you believe in Aislinn, you were willing to come with her here."

Ethan glanced at Aislinn. "Something like that."

Mark pushed a hand through his hair in a gesture that reminded Aislinn very strongly of Ethan. He exhaled gustily. "I assume you know how crazy that sounds."

Ethan put a hand on Aislinn's knee. "We try not to use the *C* word," he murmured.

She and Ethan sat side by side on a couch, while Mark faced them from a mismatched chair nearby. It was the only furniture in the room. There wasn't even a table. She got the impression that he had only recently moved into this house and hadn't yet gotten around to buying furnishings.

Focusing on his face, she said quietly, "You wouldn't have heard us out if you hadn't had some reason to think we could be telling the truth."

He shook his head slowly. "I can hardly believe I'm even entertaining the possibility, but there are a few things that make me wonder...."

"Such as?" Ethan asked, leaning forward a little on the couch.

Mark looked back at him steadily. "I can see a resemblance," he admitted. "I'd be lying if I said I didn't."

"What else?"

He drew a slightly unsteady breath and nodded toward the drawing and the envelope in Aislinn's hands. "That."

"You know who drew this?" Aislinn asked.

"I'm not sure about that. But I know who mailed it."

"Who?" Ethan demanded tensely.

Mark spread his hands. "I did."

* * *

Cassandra sat in her chair by the window, letting the late-afternoon sunlight wash over her. Her hands were folded in her lap, resting on the soft package she held there.

A slight smile played on her lips. The peacefulness she felt inside her was new, something she'd never known in her footloose, rebellious life. It felt good to finally make amends for some of the mistakes she had made. To repay some of the kindnesses that had been shown to her during the past few years.

She had brought a family back together. Something she had never been able to accomplish with her own. That had been as much her fault as anyone else's, she admitted now.

But she was most satisfied with the knowledge that Aislinn now had someone to believe in her. To accept her in a way that Cassandra herself had never been fully accepted. Someone dependable enough and strong enough to stay beside her, so she would never feel abandoned again.

Maybe if Cassandra had found someone like that in her youth…

But, no. It was too late for regrets now. She'd lived her life on her own terms, and despite the people she had hurt along the way, she knew there was no other path she could have taken. She was who she was. Who she had chosen to be. Maybe someday Aislinn would understand why it had had to be that way.

Understand…and perhaps someday forgive.

"My mother's name was Carmen Thomas," Mark said into the stunned silence that followed his announcement. "She told me my father was a soldier who died overseas. She said she had no family of her own and had never been accepted by his family. I never tried to find any of my father's family because I didn't want anything to do with people who had treated my mother badly. She raised me on her own in a little town in southern Georgia. Sometimes she worked two jobs at a time to support me."

He swallowed, his throat working with the force of it. "She was very shy. Didn't socialize much. I was pretty much her whole world. She made sure I had everything I needed. Most of what I wanted, though there wasn't a lot of extra money for luxuries. She made sure I made good grades in school, had friends and extracurricular activities to keep me out of trouble. She always wanted me to become a doctor."

"And you did," Aislinn murmured.

He nodded. "I went to medical school on loans that I've only recently finished paying back."

Again it was Aislinn who spoke, while Ethan digested what Mark was saying. "She must have been proud of you."

"She didn't live to see it," Mark answered

dully. "She died the summer after I graduated from college. A car accident."

The irony of that didn't escape any of them.

"I'm sorry," Aislinn told him. "You must have felt very much alone."

He nodded, seeming to appreciate that she understood. "Now you're telling me that she wasn't my mother at all. That she stole me from a loving family, faked her own death—and mine—and lived out the remainder of her life in hiding with me."

"That has to be a hard thing to hear."

"That's an understatement," he said on a long exhale. "I'm still not sure I believe it. Nothing about the shy, gentle woman who raised me would lead me to believe she was capable of doing something like that."

"I wouldn't believe a couple of strangers who showed up with a story like that, either," Ethan agreed. "My first thought would be that they were trying to pull some sort of scam on me. I'd demand proof. To be honest, I'm only now starting to believe you might really be Kyle. And before we go any further with this—before we tell anyone else—I think we should get that proof."

"DNA testing, you mean."

Ethan nodded. "I'll give blood. Cheek swabs. Whatever it requires."

"So will I," Mark said.

But Aislinn thought she detected a note of resignation in his voice, as if he had already predicted the results of that testing. And his heart was aching despite the brave face he was putting on for them.

"I still don't understand about this drawing," Ethan said with a frown. "You said you mailed it?"

Drawing his attention back to the present, Mark nodded. "I'm an internist with a specialty in gerontology," he explained. "The care facility where I've been practicing is filled with very wealthy people who expect regular, personalized care and can afford to pay for it. I've been paid well enough there to help me pay off my loans, though I'm planning to join a family-practice clinic in a few weeks."

He went on to tell them about a particularly intriguing patient there, a woman who never had visitors, whose past was a mystery to the entire staff but who had enough money to make their questions discreetly disappear.

"She...sees things," he added. "I don't know how, but she's told me things she couldn't possibly have known. I tried not to think about it much, but I've always wondered about her. Anyway, a few days ago she asked me to mail an envelope for her, and I agreed. I didn't know what was in it, but I recognize it as the one you're holding. I remembered that it was addressed to someone in Arkansas and that she declined to put a return address on it."

"What's her name?" Aislinn asked, holding her breath.

He hesitated. "I'm not supposed to discuss details like that. Privacy is one of the primary rules of the facility. Not to mention the law when it comes to doctor-patient confidentiality."

"I'd say the circumstances warrant some leeway," Ethan muttered.

"Her name is Cassandra Jamison," Mark revealed after another hesitation.

It didn't mean anything to either of them. But Aislinn had a feeling that it should. "How old is she?"

Mark stood abruptly. "I think you should ask her these things yourself. I'll take you to her and ask if she'll talk to you."

Aislinn knew that Mark had quite a few questions he wanted to ask her himself. His life as he had known it had just been turned upside down—and he wanted some answers.

Aislinn followed Mark and Ethan down the impeccably decorated hallways of the care facility, watching as various staff members nodded at Mark, showing little surprise at his unscheduled visit. She suspected that he had spent many hours with his patients here, that he was a dedicated doctor who took his work very seriously. It was just something she had sensed about him.

She couldn't help noticing how much he resembled Ethan. Their coloring. Their build. The way they walked. They would have their DNA tests, but as far as she was concerned, the answer was obvious.

Nerves gripped her as they neared the room in which the mysterious Cassandra lived. Something told her that this woman was as important to her as she was to Ethan and Mark.

A nurse flagged Mark down as he turned a corner. "Dr. Thomas," she said in surprise. "I was just about to call you. Have you already heard about Mrs. Jamison?"

Mark spun on one heel, while both Aislinn and Ethan went very still. The truth flooded Aislinn's mind even before the nurse explained in response to Mark's question. "She passed away a few hours ago. Dr. Marvin said it was her heart. She just…slipped away, sitting in her chair by the window."

It was at that moment that Aislinn realized who the woman who had called herself Cassandra had been.

She must have made a sound. Ethan wrapped an arm around her shoulders, while Mark talked quietly with the nurse, asking questions in medical terms Aislinn didn't completely understand. It didn't matter, she thought as she leaned into Ethan's strength. The end results were the same. Cassandra was gone.

Mark turned back to Aislinn and Ethan, his eyes as tormented as Aislinn's heart. "I don't…this was unexpected," he said, and she heard the self-blame in his voice. "She refused to go the hospital for tests, and I couldn't force her, of course, but I would have tried if I'd had any idea.…"

"This wasn't your fault," Aislinn said firmly, stepping away from Ethan to rest a hand on Mark's arm. "She didn't want you to do anything."

He squeezed the back of his neck with one hand, unable to accept her exoneration yet.

"Is there any way we can go into her room?" she asked him, knowing he would have to come to terms with this in his own way—just as she would.

He nodded. "I'll take you in. Let me get the key."

She didn't know what strings he had to pull to accomplish that, but he was back a short while later, the key in his hand.

The first thing they saw when they entered the room was the package on the dresser. It was wrapped in brown paper and had two words written in large letters on top. Staring at her own name, Aislinn put a hand to her throat.

Mark was the first to move, picking up the package and staring down at it. "I think I know what this is," he said, turning to hand it to Aislinn. "But maybe there are some answers inside, as well."

"Open it," Ethan urged when Aislinn hesitated.

Moistening her lips, she peeled the paper away to reveal a beautiful emerald-green sweater, hand-knitted in a luxuriously soft yarn. Mark nodded as if in confirmation of his guess as to the contents.

She would ask him later how he had known, but her attention was drawn then to another white envelope. This one had been enclosed with the sweater. Her name was printed on the outside in the same handwriting that had been on the one that had held the drawing she'd received in the mail.

Ethan and Mark stood nearby while Aislinn sank into a chair to draw out the three hand-written pages that had been enclosed in the envelope. They both waited while she began to read. She took her time about it, the moments ticking silently into minutes, but neither of them tried to rush her. They knew she would fill them in when she finished.

Her hands were amazingly steady when she refolded the letter, though Ethan and Mark's images swam through tears when she looked up at them. Ethan moved immediately to her side, setting a hand on her shoulder. "Are you okay?"

She nodded. "I will be."

"Was she…?"

She nodded again. "She was my mother."

This time it was Mark who had to sit down, as if his knees had suddenly given out on him. He perched on the end of the bed while he absorbed this latest stunning revelation. "I don't understand any of this," he muttered.

"I know what you mean," his brother said, remaining close to Aislinn. "I've been feeling just the way you look for the past month."

Aislinn drew a deep breath. She kept her eyes on Mark as she began to speak, afraid that looking at Ethan just then would tip her over the edge of her self-control. "I'll tell you about my mother later, but let's just say she was a free spirit who changed her identity as often as some people swap cars. I never knew her. I was raised by my grandfather and my great-aunt."

He nodded to encourage her to continue.

"According to this letter, she did a big favor for a woman thirty years ago. She regretted it soon afterward, but she didn't know how to atone for her mistake, so she put it behind her, along with quite a few other bad choices she had made during the years. And then she met you, and when she realized who you were, she saw a chance to make things right."

"Your mother was the one who picked Carmen and Kyle up on the side of that road thirty years ago?" Ethan asked in dismay, leaping to the obvious conclusion.

Aislinn nodded. "She was pretty vague about it in the letter, but apparently Carmen convinced her that Kyle was her son and that they were running from an abusive spouse. I don't know how they met exactly, but they hadn't known each other very long, apparently. They planned the whole thing in a bar. My mother said she spent a lot of time in bars back then, using the alcohol people bought for her to dull her senses and mask her pain. Carmen must have bought her a lot of drinks."

"She believed that story about the abusive spouse?" Ethan asked.

"She chose to believe it." Aislinn was able to fill in some of the blanks on her own, from the messages she got while holding the pages. Messages that hadn't been put into writing. "It seemed like a great adventure to her, and she liked the idea of herself as a rescuing heroine. She helped Carmen push her car off the side of the road and she drove her away. They drove for three days, until Carmen asked her to leave her and the baby on their own. Apparently Carmen had squirreled away enough money to set up housekeeping in a small town and begin a new life.

"By that time, Mother knew something was wrong about the story she'd been told, but she was too absorbed with her own problems to stay around and try to find out. She said she told herself that Carmen was probably just taking you away from your father. A custody-battle thing. That was easier for her to justify than the truth."

"She knew she had helped to kidnap a child, but she did nothing about it?" Mark shook his head slowly. "That just doesn't fit at all with the image of the woman I thought I knew here."

"I told you—she was very good at reinventing herself. Maybe the woman you knew wouldn't have done anything like that. I think she tried to tell my grandfather what she'd done once, but they never communicated well. He misunderstood when she talked about a little boy she had abandoned. I guess she thought she was finally setting things right by sending me the drawing."

"But how?"

"Some things are better left unasked," Ethan advised glumly. "They defy explanation."

Aislinn couldn't smile. Clearing her throat, she said, "I'll let you read the letter for yourself, Mark, but she said to tell you she was sorry. She said the same to me, actually. She said she knows it will be difficult for all of us to come to terms with the past in regard to her, but she predicted we'll all find happiness as a result of her intercession. She sounded rather pleased with herself. Maybe she was picturing herself as the heroine again."

"Aislinn."

She shook her head in response to Ethan's murmur, blinking back a fresh film of tears when she added, "She named me as her heir. Apparently there's a will on file with the management here to make it all official. So you don't have to worry about breaking patient confidentially after all, Mark. I'm fully entitled to be here, to knowing all the facts about her."

"She knew she was going to die?" Mark asked, still frowning in bewilderment.

"Yes. She said she lived life on her own terms and she left the same way."

"Now that sounds like Cassandra," he murmured, his voice thick.

Her own unsteady, Aislinn said, "Maybe you can tell me about her sometime."

He nodded as Ethan pulled Aislinn up and into his arms. Burying her face in his shoulder, she allowed herself to shed a few tears for the mother she would never know.

Because Mark's spare bedrooms were unfurnished, Aislinn and Ethan checked into a hotel not far from his house, telling him they would see him the next day. He seemed relieved to be left to himself for the remainder of the night, and Aislinn didn't blame him. He needed time and privacy in which to adjust to everything that had been dumped on him that day.

He and Ethan had parted rather awkwardly,

but both of them had seemed willing to spend time getting to know each other. Whatever relationship developed between them after that remained to be seen, but Aislinn thought they would become good friends, at least in time.

They didn't even bother getting two rooms this time. Carrying their bags inside, Ethan dumped them unceremoniously on the floor. "Are you hungry?" he asked her. "I could order room service."

She shook her head. "I couldn't eat. But order something for yourself, if you want."

"No. I'm not hungry, either." He took her hands in his, drawing her to sit beside him on the bed. "I'm so sorry, Aislinn."

She nodded. "This was the way she wanted it. She said in the letter that she wouldn't have been a good mother now, any more than she had been before. She didn't want me to look at her, knowing the things she had done, the person she had been. She didn't consider herself to be Mary Alice Flaherty anymore.

She was Cassandra Jamison, wealthy widow and kindly older woman. She wanted that to be her final identity."

"What are the odds that we all came together like this? That Joel married your friend and that your mother was the one who helped Carmen all those years ago? Hell, it makes my head hurt to think about it."

She tried to smile, though it was a weak attempt. "Mine, too. Especially since my mother left some images in there that I'm going to have to spend a while deciphering."

"What kind of images?" he asked warily.

"Just little details about her past. Flashes, I guess you would call them. Maybe she wanted me to know her a little after all."

Still holding her hand, Ethan said, "I think it's going to take all of us a while to get used to this."

"Yes. We'll have to tell your family, of course. How do you think they'll react?"

"The same way I have. With disbelief and

then stunned acceptance. My parents will be shocked but overjoyed to have Kyle back, although I guess he'll be Mark to them now. It's the only name he remembers."

"Will they blame me, you think? For my mother's part in his disappearance?"

"Why would they blame you?" he asked roughly. "You had nothing to do with it. It happened before you were born. Besides, she might have helped take him away, but you helped bring him back. They won't forget that. I won't let them."

Biting her lip, she looked up at him through her lashes. "Does that mean—"

"You were right, you know. It's been a long time since I've really trusted anyone. I've been burned a few times and I let myself get bitter. Withdrawn. Then I met you, and you asked me to trust in things that didn't even make sense. Things that went against everything I'd ever believed before."

"I know," she whispered.

"And somehow I did," he went on wonderingly. "Whether it was magic or hypnotism or plain old love at first sight, it hit me the first night we met, and I went down hard. Which didn't mean I didn't go down fighting."

She smiled through tears at that. "You fought pretty hard."

"We've known each other for a month," he reminded her. "I didn't hold out all that long."

"I didn't think I would ever meet anyone who could accept me just for who I am," she said unsteadily. "And I thought you were completely wrong for me because you were so determined not to trust me from the very start. But I went down hard that first night, also—and, trust me, I fought it, too."

"So did we both lose?"

She chuckled faintly. "I'd like to think we both won."

He kissed her lingeringly. "I love you, Aislinn."

"I love you, too."

And then he straightened, frowning. "Um, about Heather—"

"It doesn't matter."

"Yeah, it does. I want to put this behind us. And keep it forever just between us, okay?"

"Of course." She already sort of knew what he was going to tell her, but maybe he needed to put it into words.

"Joel was really busy with his residency. Didn't have a lot of time to spend with his family—or with his fiancée, Heather. She and I ended up spending some time together during the summer before they were married, just hanging around, you know. Family-type stuff. They had been together a long time, since high school, and I knew her pretty well. She was pretty amazing—beautiful, brilliant, popular. I always thought Joel was a lucky guy and hoped I would meet someone like her, since my own relationships tended to end badly."

"What happened?" she encouraged when he paused, knowing he needed to get it off his chest.

"One thing led to another—and there were some kisses," he admitted reluctantly, self-recrimination heavy in his voice. "Though I never asked her to, she told me she had considered dumping Joel for me. And then she said she changed her mind because she wanted to be a doctor's wife. I wasn't ambitious enough to be a suitable match for her."

Aislinn must have made a sound, because he spoke quickly, shaking his head. "Heather was a good person. And she loved Joel, despite her understandable last-minute doubts. She was ambitious, sure, but so was he back then. She and I agreed that nothing had really happened between us, so there was no need for Joel to ever know anything about it. We put it behind us and we never let it affect our friendship."

"Not outwardly at least," Aislinn murmured.

He sighed. "Okay, so I thought I was in love with her. After all, she died just six months after they married, and I still hadn't really had time to get over her yet, which I would have done eventually."

"But she hurt you. In a way, she betrayed both you and Joel with her flirtation. And because you felt guilty and defeated, you told yourself you weren't going to let anyone hurt you like that again."

"Maybe," he admitted. "But I know now it wasn't really love. Affection, maybe. Attraction, of course. But nothing I ever felt for her—or for anyone else—ever came close to being as powerful as what I feel for you now. For always."

"It won't be easy," she whispered, leaning into his arms. "I come with some pretty daunting complications."

"So I'm in love with a sort-of psychic. Might take some getting used to, but I've come a long way in that direction already. I'll just have to stay honest, since you would know in a heartbeat if I were trying to get away with anything."

She looked up at him with a smile. "I trust you, Ethan."

"And I trust you," he murmured, lifting her hand to his lips. "With all my heart."

It was all she had ever wanted, she thought as they sank onto the bed and into a kiss that warmed all the cold, formerly lonely places inside her. Love that came without reservations. Love that trusted. That was the greatest gift of them all.

* * * * *